CLAIMING
HIS BABY

CLAIMING HIS BABY

BY

REBECCA WINTERS

MILLS & BOON®

*First published in Great Britain 2001
Large Print edition 2002
Harlequin Mills & Boon Limited,
Eton House, 18-24 Paradise Road,
Richmond, Surrey TW9 1SR*

© Rebecca Winters 2001

ISBN 0 263 17266 X

*Set in Times Roman 16½ on 18 pt.
16-0102-48184*

*Printed and bound in Great Britain
by Antony Rowe Ltd, Chippenham, Wiltshire*

CHAPTER ONE

"HONEY? Do you have any idea how proud I am of your accomplishments? To think my daughter has established herself as a concert pianist. It's what your mother lived for..."

Groaning inwardly, Heather Sanders bowed her head. "D-do you want another cup of coffee?"

"No, thank you. You've waited on me enough this morning. In fact you've spoiled me during this visit when it should have been the other way around."

"I'm happiest when I'm home with you."

"You're just saying those kind words to make your old man happy."

"No, Daddy. It's the truth. Please, don't rush off yet." *I need to talk to you.* I *have* to talk to you.

"I'm sorry, honey, but an early start on hospital rounds means I can finish up the day ahead of schedule so I can be with you. I'd

5

like to believe your mother will be watching and listening to you play with the symphony tonight,'' came his tremulous whisper.

''I want to believe that, too. In case she is, I'll try to do Tchaikovsky justice.''

He gave her hand a gentle squeeze before letting it go. ''Your performance will be flawless, just as it always is. You're so much like her, honey.''

''Thank you, Daddy.'' Heather averted her eyes and finished the rest of her orange juice.

''I want you to know I've already made travel arrangements so that I can fly over for the performances on your tour. I'll only be able to stay a couple of days each time, but it will be worth it. Lyle Curtis has the different dates marked off to cover for me.''

''I'm so glad!'' She slid out of her chair to throw her arms around his neck. ''I love you so much.''

Dr. John Sanders was everyone's favorite obstetrician. He worked long hours and had literally buried himself in his practice since her mother had died. For him to take so much time away from his patients to be with her was some kind of miracle.

Yet thrilled as she was by his news, deep down the thought of carving out a career as a concert pianist had always been daunting to her. Though she loved the piano, the idea of devoting her life to the performance of music was already starting to hold less and less appeal. The sooner she admitted this to her father who'd sacrificed everything for her, the better.

"What are you going to do today besides practice?" he asked after standing up to give her a hug.

"I've got a lot of packing to do before I leave for New York tomorrow. Phyllis called and offered to drive me over to the concert hall early so I can warm up on the Steinway."

"Wonderful! After my last appointment, I'll come straight home and change, then join you backstage before the performance."

She flashed him a smile. "I'd love that, but I won't hold my breath. In case things get busy at the office, remember that tonight I don't play until after the intermission."

He put his hands on her shoulders. In a solemn voice he said, "Do you honestly think I'd miss the debut of my daughter's entry into the world of Rubenstein and Ashkenazy?"

"Daddy—" She shook her head. "They're legendary. Only a few pianists will ever be in their league."

"You have greatness in you, honey. This is what your mother and I dreamed of."

He kissed her forehead before leaving the dining room.

Immobilized by the growing conflict inside her, Heather stood there clinging to the chair long after she heard her father back down the driveway and leave for the hospital.

With incurious eyes, Dr. Raul Cardenas glanced out the window of the plane as it made its descent toward Salt Lake International airport. Though it was mid-June, there were still pockets of snow clinging to the highest peaks of the rugged Rocky Mountains. The sight reminded him of the Andes, and should have brought him a modicum of excitement.

But to his chagrin nothing seemed to dispel the growing discontentment he'd been feeling lately, not even the thought of seeing Evan and Phyllis again.

Urgent business had prompted this emergency visit. He needed to consult with an expert. Evan Dorney, the renowned heart surgeon who had been Raul's mentor during the last year of his surgeon's residency at University Hospital in Salt Lake, was that person.

The men had formed a fast friendship. Raul had been aware the older doctor had wanted him to stay in Salt Lake and become a partner in his thriving medical practice.

Though humbled and flattered by Evan's offer, Raul's roots tugged at him. He couldn't turn his back on his own country where doctors were desperately needed any more than he could abandon the aging aunt and uncle who'd raised him from the age of nine. Their fondest hope had been that he follow in his uncle's footsteps and become an attorney.

In the end Raul chose to be a doctor and practice medicine in the Gran Chaco of

Argentina where he felt he could make the greatest contribution, thereby thwarting his uncle's dreams and disappointing Evan.

Except for missing him and his exceptional wife, Phyllis, Raul had never regretted his decision. Determined to keep up their friendship, he'd remained close to them through phone calls and letters.

Over the intervening years the Dorneys had made four trips to Buenos Aires. Together the three of them had spent their vacations in the Andes and Patagonia. Finally Raul was coming to visit them.

Alarmed because this reunion should have generated more excitement inside of him, he was relieved when the plane had touched down so he wouldn't have to be a prisoner of his own disturbing thoughts for a while.

Unbuckling the seat belt, he shrugged into the jacket of his lightweight tan suit before starting down the aisle. The first-class section emptied fairly fast. He paused at the doorway of the waiting area to scan the crowd, then came face-to-face with a familiar pair of intelligent hazel eyes.

Except for more gray in his hair, Evan didn't seem to have changed at all. He stood tall, and his lopsided smile was still in evidence. The two men embraced.

"Evan," Raul murmured, feeling a sudden rush of emotion as a plethora of memories assailed him. This man exuded all the warmth missing in the uncle who'd done his best to take over after Raul's parents had been killed.

"You have no idea how delighted I was when you told me you were coming," the older doctor responded with heartfelt sincerity.

"Even if I'm here to ask you an enormous favor?"

"I don't care about the reason. You're here!" he cried. "That's all that matters."

"He's right," his redheaded wife spoke up as Raul caught sight of her. She held out her arms for a hug, which he readily reciprocated.

"You're beautiful as ever, Phyllis."

She wiped the tears from her eyes. "I've aged and I know it. But you—just look how handsome you are! I can't believe you're not married yet."

"I never found anyone who measured up to you, that's why."

"With all those gorgeous South American beauties?"

Raul had had several relationships with women, but he'd never been so carried away that he'd proposed marriage to any of them, much to his aunt and uncle's chagrin. Living in a city like Buenos Aires was one thing. Surviving in a tiny bush settlement like Zocheetl was something else…

"Phyllis, as I've told you on numerous other occasions, I would have to feel something earthshaking, and that hasn't happened yet."

Though busier than he'd ever been in his life, there was an aridness in his soul that nothing seemed to fill. He'd hoped a change of scene with the Dorneys might help cure what was ailing him.

"It's because you live in isolation too much of the time. If you would stay a few months in Salt—"

"Phyllis—" her husband warned. "Leave the poor man alone. He just got here after a horrendously long flight. Come on, let's grab your bags and take you home.

"I can't get there fast enough."

Within an hour he was ensconced in the Dorneys's elegant, traditional two-story house, which had been his home away from home during his residency in Salt Lake. They'd prepared his old room for him.

As soon as he'd freshened up in the en suite bathroom, he joined them downstairs in the living room. To his surprise Phyllis had changed into a blue chiffon evening gown.

"You look lovely. Where are you going all dressed up?"

"To the symphony. You've heard us speak of the Sanders—"

"Of course. They're your best friends. She's the one who died of cancer a couple of years ago, leaving a daughter."

"That's right. Last week Heather won the international Gina Bacchauer piano competition. Tonight she's performing her winning program with the Utah Symphony. I promised I'd drive over to symphony hall and be with her until she goes onstage.

"Normally I would never leave you when you've just arrived. But Heather's my goddaughter and needs me. Besides, I happen to know Evan can't wait to talk to you alone."

"I've heard of the Bacchauer," Raul interjected. "If she's that good, I'd like to attend the performance."

Evan smiled. "That's very noble of you, but if you're only in town for three days, I want to make the most of our time together."

Raul knew this event must be important to Evan as well as Phyllis. "I really would like to go to the symphony. As you both know, music is as necessary to me as breathing." He could credit his aunt and uncle for a life that included beautiful music and good books. "In fact it's probably my favorite way to enjoy an evening."

Because he spoke the truth, his voice carried the ring of conviction. Certainly the look of pleasure on their faces told its own story.

With the decision made, everyone was galvanized into action. After Phyllis placed fried chicken and potato salad on the breakfast room table, she left for the Sanders's home in her car.

Over their meal Evan urged Raul to tell him what was so important, it had caused him to leave his beloved bush.

"There's a little seven-year-old Indian boy with a strange heart condition. He's too sick to be moved from the bush hospital. I've brought his X rays with me.

"I may have done some heart surgeries because there was no one else, but I don't dare tackle anything this complicated. You'll understand when you look at the film. The parents have no money, of course. I thought that if—"

"Say no more." Evan broke in with a smile. "I'll do it. Just give me three weeks to clear my calendar."

Raul's eyes smarted. "You don't know how grateful I am. I'll pay you for the operation."

"Don't be absurd! What has life come to if we can't help people without worrying about money? I'd like to do it as long as you assist me. Phyllis will want to come, too. We've both been curious about the bush. Now will be our chance to really see it.''

"I'll have a bungalow waiting for you. In the meantime you'll need to get some booster shots.''

Evan nodded. ''It will be like old times, operating with you. I'll have you know I've never worked with a resident as brilliant as Dr. Raul Cardenas.''

Raul cleared his throat and got up from the table. ''If we're going to make the symphony, I need to get showered.''

"Go ahead. I'll clean up down here and then change. Bring those X rays with you. We'll stop at the office after the symphony and I'll take a look at them.''

Raul clapped him on the shoulder. ''Bless you, Evan.''

A half hour later they were dressed in formal attire and headed to symphony hall in Evan's car. Once inside the crowded building, an usher handed them programs and they found their seats.

"Where's Phyllis?''

"She'll probably stay backstage with Heather until John arrives."

Raul opened his program and began to read. He discovered that the second and third place winners of the piano competition would be performing before the intermission.

Soon the house lights dimmed and he sat back to enjoy the Israeli man's performance. He played the Beethoven superbly, then pleased the crowd with a George Gershwin selection. Then came the Russian contestant who did an excellent job with Chopin's Nocturne in E.

"Just wait till you hear Heather play," Evan whispered.

The corner of Raul's mouth lifted at his friend's obvious bias. When the Russian left the stage, Phyllis joined them at their seats. While the two of them conversed in private, Raul finished reading the notes about each finalist. Just before the lights dimmed after the intermission, he turned to the last page.

There he gazed on the exquisite face of Heather Sanders for the first time...

A hush fell over the audience, causing Raul to look up from his program. Everyone's concentration had centered on the winner of the Bacchauer—a young woman in black whose femininity made an impact even at the back of the hall.

She moved across the stage with a consummate grace that was stunning to watch. His gaze dropped to the program once more. The picture didn't do justice to her Nordic coloring. She seated herself at the concert grand and began her performance with a little known work of Rachmaninoff, which was one of Raul's favorite pieces.

The haunting composition was technically difficult and incredibly beautiful. Raul was secretly thrilled she'd chosen that particular work. He knew the music intimately and found himself listening for certain passages.

Her interpretation was marvelous. He felt her passion. She was doing everything right. It sent chills up his spine. Again he consulted the program.

Madre de Dios. A twenty-five-year old piano student from Juilliard and she could play like that!

She would only have been fifteen years old when he was finishing up his residency.

Evan handed him the opera glasses he and Phyllis had been sharing. Raul lifted them to his eyes. The moment the young pianist had made her appearance onstage he'd been inordinately curious about her, wondering if he'd imagined the perfection of her face and figure.

Perhaps it was a trick of light and the long black dress she was wearing, but her shoulder-length hair looked like a spray of gossamer, as if it had an inherent ability to shimmer.

Her well-shaped head was bent over the keyboard so he could only perceive small glimpses of the total person—the hint of high cheekbones, a generous mouth and softly rounded chin.

Moving lower, he noticed her hand span was not excessive because she wasn't a tall woman. But her fingers were strong, her touch, eloquent. He didn't want to give up the glasses when Phyllis reached for them again.

She began her second number, Tchaikovsky's Second Piano Concerto, a lesser known work than the First. So many pi-

anists failed at this particular piece, but she
revealed a depth of emotion and power that
transcended the mere mechanics and ended up
giving a sterling performance. Raul found himself holding his breath.

When the last note had been played, there
was a reverent pause before the audience burst
into applause. Raul got to his feet along with
Phyllis and Evan. The clapping reached a cres-
cendo with shouts of bravo. It didn't end despite the several graceful bows she made.

Someone thrust a bouquet of flowers in her
arms. The conductor held her hand high for the
audience. Another thunderous ovation continued for several more minutes. Even without
the benefit of opera glasses, he felt the radiance
of her smile.

"Give me your keys," Raul murmured to
Evan who was plainly ecstatic over his goddaughter's performance. "While you go backstage to congratulate her, I'll bring the car
around in front of the concert hall and pick you
up."

"Come with us."

Raul shook his head. "Not this time. Take as long as you want."

Evan dropped the keys in his outstretched hand. "Thank you," he said in a thick-toned voice and hurried down the aisle after his wife.

This was one time Raul didn't want to intrude on their private moment. In truth, he had no desire to meet Heather Sanders for the simple reason that she was the embodiment of everything he found attractive in a woman, not only physically, but emotionally.

That kind of complication he didn't need in his life. Coming to Salt Lake had been a necessity. On Monday he'd be flying back to South America. The sooner he left, the better.

But in his heart of hearts, he couldn't deny that something of tremendous significance had happened to him during her performance. Though it had only been a moment out of time, he was already feeling unmistakable stirrings. The type that needed to be repressed at all costs.

Heather heard her dad's beeper go off while they were in the car driving home from the symphony. As soon as he started talking on the cell phone, she knew it was a patient who'd gone into labor. Before he clicked off, he told the woman to meet him at the hospital.

There went any hope of spending her last evening with him for at least a month. Being an obstetrician's daughter, she was used to him leaving for the hospital at a moment's notice. But tonight she needed him.

Despite her performance, which she felt was the best she'd ever given, she felt emotionally drained. She wanted to talk to him about her life and her concerns. Yet at the same time she was nervous because she didn't know how he would react. The last thing she would ever want to do was hurt him or cause him grief.

"Honey?"

His voice jerked her from her torturous thoughts. She turned her head in his direction. "I know. You have a patient who needs you."

"I'm sorry. Hopefully I won't be long. You heard Phyllis. She asked us to come over, so I'll drive you there right now and join you later. I don't want you to be alone, not after the fabulous performance you gave tonight."

Heather didn't know what she wanted.

"It was a good thing I stayed in the wings," he continued, unaware of her turmoil. "I was able to break down without anyone noticing that your old dad was the proudest father on the planet. A lot of important people were there tonight. Everyone gave you rave reviews. I could have told them you're an incredible daughter as well as a pianist."

"The feeling's mutual, Daddy. I don't know how I was lucky enough to be born to you and Mom. You both gave me a beautiful life." Her voice trembled.

He reached across to pat her hand. "Honey—you sound like everything's over when it's only just begun. That must be your exhaustion talking."

Maybe it was.

Maybe that was what was wrong with her.

She needed sleep and lots of it.

Now that the pressure of performing in her own home city was over, she would probably be able to let go of her anxiety.

"Heather?" her father prodded.

"You're right, Daddy. I *am* tired."

"Tell Phyllis you need to lie down and put your feet up."

"That sounds divine."

A few minutes later he turned into the Dorneys's driveway. She leaned over to give him a kiss on the cheek. "Hurry back."

"You know I will."

She got out of the car and dashed up the steps of the house. Phyllis already had the door open and drew Heather inside.

"Oh, no!" she cried when she saw the car drive off.

"There was an emergency. Daddy said he wouldn't be long."

"How many times have we heard that?"

They smiled at each other in total understanding before Phyllis shut the door. "So—what does the newest and brightest star on the concert stage want to do first?"

"Would you mind terribly if I just lie down for a while?"

Phyllis eyed her with concern. "Do you even have to ask? Can I bring you something?"

"No. Nothing. But thank you so much any-way. Where's Evan?"

"He had to stop by the office to look over some X rays, but he'll be here shortly. You go on in the study and make yourself comfortable on the couch."

"Thank you, Phyllis. You've been wonder-ful to me."

"You're like the daughter I never had. I'm the one who's lucky."

Fighting tears, Heather gave her a hug, then headed for the study. As at home in the Dorney house as her own, she wandered into the book-lined den where she'd often practiced on their piano. Stepping out of her black high-heeled sandals, she placed a cushion at one end of the sofa, then lay down and closed her eyes.

She was always tired after a performance, but it was her troubled mental and emotional state that made her body feel like it weighed a thousand pounds.

When Raul opened the French doors of the study looking for the newspaper, he was stunned to discover Heather Sanders lying full-length on the long green velvet couch still wearing her floor-length black dress. Talk about Sleeping Beauty...

The noise brought her awake because her eyelids fluttered open. But she gazed at him for so long without saying anything, he realized she'd been in a deep sleep for quite some time.

He stood a few feet away from her, yet he was close enough to be fascinated by a pair of electrifying blue eyes watching him out of inky black lashes.

There were lakes high in the Andes their exact color. Raul had camped along their shores, mesmerized by the brilliant hue of those still, deep waters. Combined with her northern European blond coloring, the contrast took his breath.

''Ms. Sanders? I didn't know anyone was in here or I would never have disturbed you.''

A red blush crept up her neck and face as she came to a sitting position and swung her feet to the floor. The imprint of the hand upon which she'd been lying was still visible on her velvety cheek, like a young child's. Yet there was a womanly thrust of curves revealed beneath the material draping her gorgeous figure.

"I didn't know you were a houseguest," came her quiet response. Phyllis hadn't said a word to her about Dr. Cardenas being in Salt Lake. Why? "My father dropped me off here on his way to the hospital. I only meant to rest for a minute."

Her eyes darted to the clock on the table. "I can't believe it's almost one o'clock."

"After the events of this evening, your fatigue is perfectly understandable," he murmured. His gaze returned to the white-gold of her hair. Earlier he hadn't been able to get a good enough look at her from his seat in the symphony hall.

With some disgust he realized that part of the reason he'd been prowling around the Dorney house for something to read stemmed from the fact that her image had been haunting him since she'd made her appearance onstage.

He didn't particularly care if his intimate perusal embarrassed her. The combination of those sapphire orbs against the creamy richness of such smooth skin drew his attention until he couldn't look anywhere else. He had the overwhelming urge to put his lips to the hollow of her throat where a pulse throbbed.

She was at a distinct disadvantage because her high heels lay next to the piano and her toes were curling in distress from his scrutiny. This reaction pleased him no end.

During the concert she'd been in total possession of herself. He liked the idea that he'd caught her off balance. The corners of his mouth lifted as he reached down and handed them to her.

"Your shoes, Ms. Sanders. Put them on if it will make you feel less vulnerable. But if you want my opinion, I prefer you just the way you are."

The bloom on her cheeks turned to flame. "Thank you, Dr. Cardenas." She took the heels from him. With a dignity he admired, she slipped her well-shaped feet into them.

"You're welcome."

His smile widened as she stood up. He could sense she wanted to arrange her hair and make sure her dress was in place. All those little things women do to feel at their best.

But she did neither. She wasn't going to give him the satisfaction. That tiny spark of defiance intrigued him.

"Since we both appear to know each other without having been formally introduced, let's dispense with last names, shall we, Heather?" he suggested in a silky voice.

Her chin lifted. "Since you haven't been to Salt Lake for a decade, and probably won't return for another, I can't see that it's of consequence either way."

The conversation had taken an odd twist. He was no longer amused. "Why do I have the feeling there was something personal in your remark?"

She had the grace to blush, and finally deigned to look at him. "I'm sorry. That was very rude of me." He watched her take a little breath. "It's just that you must have made Evan so happy by finally coming to visit, it will seem cruel when you have to go away again. The stretches between their vacations with you have been hard on him."

Her honesty was sobering. "I regret that it took me so long. My seeming indifference to the Dorneys in the past has obviously condemned me. But I assure you that were it not for a very sick patient, nothing could drag me away now.''

Once again he found himself studying the contrast of dark brows and lashes against her extreme fairness.

She shook her head. ''It's none of my business. The important thing is, you *did* come. Evan will be a new man.''

His dark brows furrowed. ''I don't think I understand.''

''I'm not certain I do.'' A sad smile came and went. ''But for reasons best known to Evan, he has always wanted you to live in Salt Lake, maybe go into practice with him.'' She bit her lip, drawing Raul's attention to the enticing mouth he desired to taste for himself.

''Apparently he wanted to be a kind of surrogate father to you.'' She rushed on. ''It really devastated him when you chose to go back to South America.''

Raul was incredulous at her frank speaking. Rubbing the back of his neck, he gazed at her through veiled eyes.

"Thank you, Heather. You've given me new insight into his feelings. Be assured mine run every bit as deeply. But I couldn't turn my back on the aunt and uncle who took care of me after my parents died in an earthquake."

She moaned. "How devastating for you."

"It was. I won't lie about that. But the experience highlighted my country's need for more doctors. There weren't enough to take care of all the injured. That's when I determined to become a doctor and make a contribution. Those are the reasons I couldn't accept Evan's offer, however much I might have wanted to at the time."

Her eyes searched his with an intensity that held him spellbound. "You're not at all what I expected," she blurted as if she couldn't help herself.

CHAPTER TWO

RAUL'S head reared back. "You're *totally* un-expected."

Her intrusion into his carefully planned life had come as a tremendous shock. "You deserved to win the Bacchauer. I would have given you my vote on the strength of the Rachmaninoff alone."

"Thank you," she responded with a warm smile.

Dios. Her charm fell over him like an invisible cloak, enveloping him so completely, he was helpless to throw it off.

"It's a difficult piece of music. Mother was my first teacher. She told me if I could learn to play it the way it should be played, then I would be ready to contemplate a career on the concert stage."

He nodded his dark head. "She was right. An amateur shouldn't touch it. In truth, it's one of my favorite compositions. Would it offend you to learn that when you first sat down to play, I didn't expect to hear genius?''

''Hardly that. But I'm glad you enjoyed the concert, and I think it tells me you're an authentic music lover. Do you play?''

''Let's just say I learned the fundamentals a long time ago. I prefer to sit back and listen to the experts. Your performance tonight was flawless. I could listen to you indefinitely.''

I could do many things to you indefinitely...

''You're very kind.'' A mischievous expression made her remarkable eyes sparkle. ''I, too, have a confession. When you said you were in the audience tonight, I imagined your appearance was more in the line of duty to make Evan and Phyllis happy.''

Raul's lips twitched. ''It's gratifying to realize you don't know every thing about me yet. Someone once told me I had no heart. Perhaps it's true. But whatever beats there responded completely to the music I heard tonight. Music has been known to tame the wild beast.''

''I wouldn't go so far as to call you a wild beast.''

One black brow quirked. "If I told you some of the thoughts that have passed through my mind since your performance, you'd be forced to take those words back."

A puzzled look crossed over her expressive face. "I don't understand."

"It's my way of saying that I'm attracted to you. To be frank, attracted is a very mild word. If I were being totally honest, I would tell you that I'd like to take you away to some isolated haven where I could make love to you for weeks on end."

For once the telltale blush didn't appear. Quite the opposite in fact. Slowly she turned away from him without saying anything. Anticipating her instinct to flee from a predator, he moved directly behind her and put his hands on her shoulders, preventing her from leaving the room altogether.

He could feel her tremble. "I've shocked you, Heather. I'm sorry."

There was a long silence. "No, you're not," she whispered at last.

At her candor, he sucked in his breath. "You're right. I'm not."

Suppressing the urge to slide his arms around her waist and draw the voluptuous warmth of her body against his, he removed his hands and stepped away.

"Whether you believe me or not, I've never said that to another woman. Not on a first meeting or otherwise." He raked a hand through his hair. "This seems to be a night for honesty on both our parts."

His comment brought her blond head around. The stunned look on her lovely face let him know she was equally aware of the powerful chemistry between them.

"How long are you going to be in Salt Lake?"

"For two more days. When are you returning to New York?"

She smoothed a silky strand of hair away from her heated cheek. "Noon tomorrow."

He shifted his weight. "The timing couldn't be worse."

Their gazes locked. To her credit, she didn't try to pretend that she'd misunderstood. "You're flying back to Argentina?"

"Yes."

"To the bush."

"That's where I live and head a small hospital."

"Were you born there?"

"No. Buenos Aires."

Her chest rose and fell sharply. "What is it really like?"

Raul took his time answering. "It's a god-forsaken wilderness of disease, heat and humidity."

"But you love it," she murmured.

He nodded. "The same way you love the piano."

There was a perceptible hardening of her delicate jaw. "The two aren't comparable."

Folding his arms he said, "I think they are. Music is your life. The bush is mine."

Raul wasn't destined to hear her response because Evan walked in on them.

"It looks as if you two are already acquainted." He glanced first at Raul, then Heather. "Your dad just pulled up in the driveway. Phyllis sent me to tell you she has a post-midnight snack waiting in the dining room."

"I'm glad he's back. I'll go help her put everything on." She left the room in a hurry. Raul followed Evan out of the study, but his eyes remained on her retreating figure.

In the hallway Evan introduced Raul to Heather's father. One glance at John Sanders and Raul realized he'd bequeathed his good looks and coloring to his daughter. It was Heather's mother who had endowed her with such an amazing musical talent.

The three men moved through the house to the kitchen. Phyllis had prepared a veritable feast of salads, cold cuts and French bread. Evan told everyone to be seated. Soon they were helping themselves to the delicious food.

"What are your plans after you return to New York?" Raul watched Heather over the rim of his coffee cup, waiting for the answer to the question that had been burning him alive.

"She's scheduled to go on tour," John spoke up unexpectedly.

Phyllis eyed Raul. "It's a shame she can't stay home for a while and play on the new concert grand she was given as her prize for winning the Bacchauer."

"That sounds like the perfect gift for you, Heather."

She put down her fork. "I'm afraid I won't be able to enjoy it for a long time."

Her father frowned. "Why ever not? I plan to ship it to New York."

"I'm leaving it at home."

"Nonsense.

"Daddy—I already told you I'm giving you that piano in honor of all you and mother did for me. The Knabe in New York serves me perfectly well when I'm there. Have you forgotten I'll be staying with Franz at his summer home to get ready for the tour?"

"Who's Franz?" Raul wanted to know, experiencing an irrational dislike of any man who would be on such an intimate basis with her.

"My teacher."

"Where does he live?"

"In Vienna. I'll be flying there next week."

The need to do something physical with his negative energy had Raul reaching for another piece of bread.

"Franz has arranged for her concert tour," John revealed with visible pride. "So far he's lined up London, Brussels, Paris, Rom—"

"R-Rome's not confirmed yet," Heather stammered before pushing herself away from the table. "Excuse me for a minute please." As she disappeared into the kitchen, Raul saw John flash Phyllis a bewildered look.

"What was that all about?"

"She was so tired after the performance, she literally collapsed on the couch. But I admit she's not reacting in her normal way.

"I noticed that, too." Evan wiped the corner of his mouth with a napkin. "I guess we'll never understand the kind of pressure she's been under." Suddenly his gaze found Raul's. "She reminds me of someone with a mild case of shock."

No doubt Evan had felt the tension in the study when he'd walked in on the two of them a little while ago. With that inquiring mind of his, it was only natural he would speculate over what had gone on between Heather and his newly arrived houseguest in his absence.

Raul could have enlightened everyone about her mental state. He'd been deeply disturbed by their encounter and suffered the same reaction, but could do nothing about it. She was leaving for the East Coast in less than ten hours. By next week she would be in Austria. *Dios.*

"Phyllis? I can't thank you enough for watching out for Heather, let alone preparing this wonderful meal. But now it's late for everyone, and I need to take my daughter home if she's going to get any more sleep and still make it to the airport on time."

If Raul were a wise man, he would avoid temptation by saying good-night to Dr. Sanders, then plead fatigue and disappear upstairs. But he'd never felt less like sleeping.

In all honesty, he'd never felt so out of control in his life. It was a feeling totally foreign to him.

Gathering some of the dishes, he headed for the kitchen where he found Heather at the sink swallowing a couple of painkillers with a glass of water.

When he put the plates on the counter, their eyes met in a long, unsmiling regard.

"Your father's ready to take you home."

"Daddy's dead on his feet and should have been in bed ages ago. After your long flight, I'm sure you're exhausted, too. For the Dorneys' sake, I'm glad you came," she said in a shaky voice.

Her remark brought him up short. "But not for your sake."

She looked away. "I—I didn't mean that the way it sounded."

"Then what did you mean?" he demanded.

"Nothing," she whispered. "I guess this is goodbye. Good luck to you, Dr. Cardenas. I hope you find all is well when you return home."

If she'd had a lifetime to prepare what to say to him, she couldn't have come up with anything as calculated to destroy the last vestiges of his peace of mind, because Raul had the gut feeling he would never find contentment at home again. Not now that he knew a certain woman with hot blue eyes and gossamer hair existed somewhere else on the planet…

"I don't need to wish you luck. You're very gifted, Heather. If you play every concert the way you played tonight, you'll be a world sensation."

"Thank you," she answered woodenly.

As if on cue, her father opened the door connecting the dining room and the kitchen. Gut instinct told Raul that Dr. Sanders didn't like him.

"Ready, honey?"

"I'm coming."

"Dr. Cardenas—" Her father nodded to him as he put an arm around Heather's shoulders. "It was very nice making your acquaintance."

"The pleasure was all mine, Dr. Sanders."

"Enjoy this time with Evan and Phyllis."

But don't get any ideas about seeing my daughter again?

Raul could read the other man's mind.

"I already am. Goodbye."

His eyes swept over Heather's unforgettable face one more time before she was whisked from the kitchen and his life.

When they'd gone, an emptiness stole through him. In the past few hours he'd felt more emotion than he had since he was nine years old. But the pain of losing his parents was completely different than the kind of pain he was suffering now.

This was agony in a dimension he couldn't begin to describe. In truth, the intensity of the loss he was feeling staggered him.

Dios.

After thirty-seven years *it was finally happening.*

"Heather? Wait up!"

No. Not Todd.

She didn't want to talk to anyone right now. If she pretended she hadn't heard him, she might just get away with losing him once she'd entered the practice hall.

"Hey—" The blond pianist from Michigan caught up to her inside the doors. "I've been waiting to congratulate you on winning the Bacchauer. Everyone's talking about it. You're famous!"

"I don't think so, Todd, but it's very nice of you to say so." She continued walking down the hall to the cubicle where she practiced. He kept up with her.

"Later on tonight I'd like to take you out for a spaghetti dinner to celebrate. Do you have plans?"

She pulled the keys out of her purse and unlocked the door, then looked over at him. "I'm afraid I do. It's already three o'clock, and I need to put in at least six hours of work, but I appreciate the thought."

He rocked back on his heels with his hands in his pockets. "Tomorrow night then?" His hopeful expression increased her guilt.

Heather had only been with Todd in group situations. She'd never had a romantic interest in him or any other man. It had taken the trip to Salt Lake for her to finally understand why.

Something earthshaking had happened to her there. Something she couldn't talk about to anyone.

"I can't, Todd. I'm sorry. Day after tomorrow I leave for Vienna and need to get in as much practice as possible before I go. Thank you anyway, though.'' She went inside and shut the door, locking it to make sure no one else bothered her.

This was the only place she could be alone. She shared a room at the residence hall with another female student, but there was no peace in the dorm, especially since the news had gotten around about her winning the competition.

Everyone had been wonderful to her, and their praise meant a great deal. Yet the continual talk about her promising future on the concert circuit was choking her.

Free to give in to her emotions where no one was witness, she sank down on the piano bench and buried her face in her hands. Today was Monday. *He was in the air now, winging his way back to South America.* She could hardly bear it.

Ever since he'd walked into the Dorneys' study, she'd been haunted by his image, the sensation of his hands on her shoulders. She'd never be able to forget what he'd said to her, not when she'd felt the same way about him.

I'm attracted to you. To be frank attracted is a mild word. To be totally honest, I'd like to take you away to some isolated haven where I could make love to you for weeks on end.

"I've got to get you out of my mind, Raul," she whispered in agony to the empty room. "*I've got to*. Otherwise, I don't know how I'll be able to go on living."

Wiping the moisture from her eyes with the backs of her hands, she plunged into her scales, ferociously attacking them in an effort to drive one Dr. Cardenas from her consciousness.

The cubicles of Juilliard's practice hall seemed to be full of students. As Raul entered the building, music surrounded him at every step. He looked on the placards outside each door, but some of them didn't have names. So far he hadn't found the one he was searching for.

If he didn't make contact with Heather, no one would be the wiser. It was probably just as well. She represented forbidden fruit. Any kind of relationship with her would be *vetoed* by her father. Raul had already been warned off by Dr. Sanders' behavior in Evan's kitchen.

As for Heather, he couldn't imagine what kind of reception he'd get if they met again, not after certain things he'd said to her in private. Those words had poured from his psyche without his volition, shocking him as much as they'd immobilized her.

When he didn't see her name anywhere, he decided he'd made a mistake in coming here. Living on campus at Lincoln Center in the heart of New York, she could be in a dozen different places. At this point it would be wisest to head back to the airport where he would wait to board his flight to Buenos Aires.

But as he turned to walk back the way he'd come, he spotted a blond male dressed in shirt-sleeves and shorts leaning over a drinking fountain. Obviously he was a student here. On impulse, Raul approached him.

"Excuse me, but I'm looking for a pianist named Heather Sanders. She's a gilt blond with blue eyes. Do you know her?"

The younger man lifted his head. As he stared hard at Raul, the glint of hostility flashed in his eyes. "Who are you?"

The guy was so painfully obvious, Raul had to fight back a few choice retorts. But on another level he was relieved the younger man was watching out for her. A stranger up to no good could be loitering around here, lying in wait for a woman like Heather. Possibly that was the reason she hadn't put a sign outside her door.

"My name is Dr. Cardenas. I'm an acquaintance of hers from Salt Lake. Do you know if she's in the building?"

The words "Salt Lake" must have done the trick. After a short pause, "That's her practice room," the guy said, inclining his head toward the door opposite them. "But I wouldn't disturb her right now if I were you."

Raul's pulse rate tripled. Heather *was* here. His eyes closed tightly for a moment.

"She's getting ready to go on tour," the man continued to inform Raul as if he were Heather's personal press secretary and watchdog rolled into one. "The best thing to do would be to leave a message. I'll see that she gets it."

I'll just bet you will. "I appreciate that, but my plane leaves too soon to wait for her to contact me. Thank you for the information."

Ignoring the younger man's glower, Raul walked across the hall to the door and listened. She was working on the Brahms Piano Concerto Number One, another favorite of his. Feelings stirred inside him. He knocked.

If Heather had thought she could exorcise Raul Cardenas from her thoughts with a grueling practice schedule, she was very much mistaken. To her consternation, the increased isolation in the cubicle tended to make her concentrate on him to the exclusion of anything or anyone else.

When a knock came at the door, she ignored it. Hopefully the person on the other side would go away and leave her alone. Surely Todd had gotten the message and wouldn't dare bother her now.

The knocking persisted.

Almost angrily she pounded out the last set of chords and jumped up from the piano bench, pulling her T-shirt down over her shorts. With the light of battle in her eyes, she undid the lock and opened the door.

There was instant stillness as she gazed up into the sun-bronzed face and midnight eyes that had scorched her with their intimate perusal in Evan's study three nights ago.

Without her high heels, his six-foot-two physique seemed even taller, his black hair curlier in the humidity. He was the most gorgeous male she'd ever beheld.

Heather held on to the door. She was afraid that if she let go, she would sink to the carpeted floor. There were so many questions she wanted to ask, she couldn't think of one. Fear that he'd sought her out because of some family crisis prevented her from saying anything at all.

Raul was still trying to recover his breath. He'd been living with the image of her in the long black dress she'd worn to play with the symphony. He wasn't prepared for this side of her in a ponytail and bare legs. She wore no makeup, and looked utterly desirable.

"Your bodyguard out here in the hall seems to think you wouldn't want to be disturbed. Is that true?" he inquired silkily.

Bodyguard? Her delicate brows frowned. "Oh—y-you must mean Todd," she said when she could finally manage to talk. Beyond Raul's broad shoulder she could see him glaring at the two of them from across the hall. "He's just another student here."

Raul stared at her through shuttered eyes. "*He* doesn't seem to think so."

Heather was still incredulous that instead of being halfway to South America by now, Raul was standing outside her practice room.

"Has something happened to my father or the Dorneys? Is that why you're here?" she asked anxiously.

He rested one hand against the doorjamb. "The problem is a little closer to home, Ms. Sanders. I'm afraid something's happened to *me*."

She shook her head. "I don't understand."

"What would you say if I told you I changed my flight because I expressly wanted to see you again?"

Warmth started from Heather's toes and crept up her body to her face until she felt white-hot.

"I—I thought you were on your way to Argentina."

"I am. I have about twenty minutes before I must leave for the airport."

No!

Smothering a groan she cried, "Then why did you bother to come at all?"

She heard him take a deep breath. "Maybe to find out if you were merely a figment of my fertile imagination."

Feeling light-headed, Heather didn't know where to look. "You shouldn't have come."

"You're right." His voice grated. "But for once in my life I did something totally against my better judgment."

She moistened her lips in a nervous gesture. "Th-this is too soon after Salt Lake."

Her honesty was as disarming now as it was the night they met. Raul bit out an epithet before raking an unsteady hand through his hair. He straightened to his full, intimidating height.

"Shall I let you get back to your practicing?"

"No—" she blurted, absolutely frantic he would walk away and leave her more desolate than ever.

His black eyes narrowed on her mouth. "Where can we go and be alone, Heather?"

Though they weren't touching, he could feel her tremble.

"Right here."

She'd finally whispered the words he'd been desperate to hear. Raul knew that if he went into that room, his whole life was going to change. He had the gut feeling she knew it, too. It was as if they could read each other's minds.

He hesitated, giving her a chance. For what, he didn't know exactly. She simply stood there, waiting...

Unable to help himself, he moved inside, taking the irreversible step. As he closed the door behind him, he noted the stunned expression on the young man's face.

Raul fastened the lock, then turned to her. "You know what I want to do."

"Yes," came the aching reply. "It's all I've been able to think about."

"Then come here to me, *muchacha,*" Raul begged.

She stepped slowly into his arms, raising her mouth blindly for his kiss. He lifted her off the floor to mold her beautiful body to his, but nothing in his imagination had prepared him for the experience of touching and tasting Heather Sanders.

Her overwhelming response swept away all barriers, leaving Raul the one who was trembling from the passion she'd aroused. He'd heard it in her music, had spent sleepless nights dreaming of unleashing it in his arms. The reality was beyond his comprehension.

Together they began to move and breathe as one flesh. He wanted to know all there was to know about her, and could no more stop what was happening than she could.

Heather had never experienced this kind of ecstasy before. The few kisses she'd exchanged with the boys she'd dated had nothing to do with this mindless rapture. Raul had awakened an insatiable hunger in her. She never wanted this giving and taking to end.

She moaned aloud when he tore his lips from hers and buried his face in the silken sheen of her hair. His breathing had grown shallow.

"*Madre de Dios*. I want you, Heather. I want you so badly I could swallow you alive." He crushed her closer. "How am I going to walk away from you, *amorada?*"

Still caught up in a state of sensual euphoria, his question didn't register all at once. But when it did, it might as well have been a dagger plunged to the very core of her being. Through sheer strength of will she stopped raining kisses on his face and pulled completely out of his arms.

Shaking like a leaf in the wind she cried, "How can you tell me you want me, and then ask me that question in the same breath?"

His features hardened, making him look older. "How can I not? We have no future. I had no right to touch you. If your father had any idea I had come here—"

Heather grasped the corner of the piano for support. "I—I think you'd better go now." She forced the words from lips swollen by his kisses. "You'll miss your plane."

He felt as if he'd been running for miles and couldn't catch his breath. "I made a grave mistake in coming."

Her proud chin lifted. "If you're worried on my account, please don't be. We've both satisfied a craving. Th-that's all it was."

Raul shook his head. "That's the first dishonest thing you've said since I met you." His face darkened with lines. "I wish to God it were the truth."

Heather held her ground. "In time we'll work each other out of our systems. Living on different continents will help."

His black eyes glittered dangerously. "You don't believe that any more than I do."

"I won't have an affair with you."

There was a long pause. "You have a lot to learn about me, Heather. The only way I'd take you is in holy wedlock and that possibility is out of the question."

Another stab wound.

Naturally a thirty-seven-year old doctor who'd lived in the bush without a wife all this time had no plans to acquire one at this late date. Heather didn't want to hear anymore.

"Please go, Raul."

"You know you don't want me to."

"Now what are you saying?" she cried out in abject frustration.

His hands balled into fists. "So help me, I wish I knew. My life is not a conventional one. Your career on the concert stage is just beginning. You've a glorious future ahead of you. A normal courtship is out of the question for reasons too obvious to bother discussing.

"An affair with a weekend here or there every couple of months couldn't possibly satisfy either one of us. The only solution to our problem would be to get married at some point, or never see each other again.

"If I asked you to be my wife, you would have to walk away from the concert stage and never look back. After certain things Evan shared with me, I don't even want to think about what it would do to your father.

"I'll tell you right now, I'm a possessive man. I couldn't share you with anything or anyone. If you and I were to marry, I'd want you with me every night."

At this juncture Heather couldn't take it all in, and sank down on the piano bench.

"My life's work is in the bush. You would have to come to my world. There could be no compromise. In other words, Heather, I'd be doing all the taking, and you'd end up hating me.

"The environment is so hostile, it's difficult to find health workers from my own country willing to work in the bush hospital. Someone like you would never survive there."

She jumped up from the bench. "You don't know that!"

"The hell I don't!" His chest heaved. "Much as I might want you for my wife, I couldn't risk robbing you of the life you were meant to live. You have a unique gift to give to the world. I would never ask you to make such a sacrifice."

Before she could comprehend it, he'd undone the lock and turned the handle of the door.

"Forgive the intrusion. It will never happen again."

He meant what he said. In about one second he was going to walk away from her and she really would have seen the last of him. She couldn't let that happen.

"Don't go, Raul!"

He wheeled around, grim-faced.

"Stay until tomorrow," she begged. "If this is all we can ever have of each other, then let's at least spend this one night together."

His powerful body tautened. "If you're saying what I think you're saying, then you don't have any idea what you're inviting. I know in my gut you've never been with a man before."

"Are you going to use the fact that I'm a virgin against me?" came her angry cry. "A few minutes ago you told me you wanted me."

She felt his smoldering gaze.

"More than you could possibly imagine."

"I want you, too," she declared from her soul. "Please, Raul. Make love to me tonight. I've been aching for you."

He seemed to pale beneath his tan. "You'll regret it tomorrow."

"If I can't be with you tonight, then the rest of my tomorrows will never have the same meaning for me again."

"Don't say that," he ground out.

"Why?" she fired at him. "Because you know it's true?"

She could sense the battle going on inside of him.

"You're an innocent, Heather."

"Give me some credit, Dr. Cardenas. I'll be twenty-six next month. Every close friend of mine is already married. In some cases they've started families. Since marriage doesn't seem to be in my future any more than yours, I guess in your eyes that's supposed to preclude my having a personal life at all."

She turned sharply away from him, fearing he would see her tears. "Just go—"

Miraculously she felt his arms slide around her hips from behind. His touch dissolved her bones.

"You want this night together?" he murmured against the side of her neck. "So do I, *amorada*. Let's not waste another second of it destroying each other. I know a place an hour from here where I can love you in total comfort and privacy."

Raul— Her heart leaped for joy as she twisted around to meet his descending mouth.

CHAPTER THREE

WHILE Dr. Sanders and Franz sat talking in the suite her father had booked for them, Heather looked out the hotel window. The rain in Brussels hadn't let up for three days.

Apparently this was typical for mid-September, but she hated the dark sky. Inclement weather made everything so somber. It all went to deepen the depression she'd been in throughout her concert tour of Europe. Franz hadn't said a word, but she was her own harshest critic and hadn't been pleased with her playing.

Since the unforgettable night she'd spent in Raul's arms, she'd waited for a phone call or a letter asking her to meet him somewhere. Anything to let her know he couldn't live without her and wanted her to join him in the bush. Secretly she'd been preparing for that eventuality.

61

But after three months of quiet on his end, she feared that no matter how much pleasure they'd given each other, he'd stuck to his original decision to never see her again.

The silence was killing her. She couldn't fathom a future without him. Now that she'd performed her last concert for the season, she was fast reaching a crisis state because nothing sounded good to her anymore. If she couldn't be with Raul, she didn't want anything else.

No longer associated with Juilliard, if she chose to use New York as a base between tours her agent was in the midst of planning for her, that meant finding an apartment. Her father was eager to help her. But New York had never felt like home to her. It never would.

Once again Franz and his wife, who lived in Linz, had offered their summer house in Vienna as a semipermanent residence. She was welcome to stay there for the next year or two while she was on the concert circuit.

Neither option appealed. She would prefer to return to Salt Lake and live with her father. More than anything she wanted to stop playing concerts altogether and give music lessons while she took care of him. But he would never understand, which was why she was afraid to broach the subject.

''Honey? Come finish your breakfast and tell us what you've decided to do. The limousine will be taking me to the airport before long.''

She returned to the sitting area and reached for a cup of tea, the only thing she felt wouldn't make her sick right now. Ten weeks ago the doctor had started her immunization shots including yellow fever, and she'd begun taking antimalaria pills. Throughout that time she'd had periods of nausea, which had robbed her of an appetite.

''If it's all right with you, Franz, I'd like to stay in Vienna, at least for the time being.''

He slapped his hands on his knees before jumping to his feet. ''Excellent! I have dozens of invitations for you to perform recitals around Salzburg and Innsbruck. They will boost your career much faster if you stay in Europe as I had hoped. We'll talk everything over at the end of the week when I'm in Vienna.

"Now if you'll excuse me, I have more business to take care of. John? A safe flight home." He shook her father's hand, then turned to Heather.

"As for you, young lady, you've already been given a key to the apartment. The house-keeper will be expecting you and have your room ready."

"Thank you, Franz." They hugged each other before he left the suite.

"I'm glad that's settled," her father murmured after Heather's teacher had disappeared. "I'll sleep better knowing he and his wife will be keeping an eye on you."

He went into the other room for his suitcase. She followed him. "Daddy?"

"Yes, honey?"

"You were with mother constantly toward the end. What did she say exactly a-about my future?"

"That she hated leaving you at such a vulnerable time in your life. I promised her I would see to it every dream was fulfilled. Somewhere in heaven she's smiling down at her beautiful daughter who is bringing pleasure to so many thousands of people. Last night's performance of the Beethoven was a case in point.''

He shrugged into his top coat. ''There. I'm ready. Come on and walk me downstairs to the limo.'' They left the hotel room arm in arm.

''You never did tell me why Phyllis and Evan didn't join you for this last concert. I thought they were going to come.''

''They would have, but the young boy Evan had operated on at the bush hospital several months ago developed complications. He had to fly down there a few weeks back to do another operation, so he couldn't take any more time off.''

Evan had been with Raul again? Why hadn't her father mentioned a word of it to her?

Her heart began to hammer. ''H-how is Dr. Cardenas?''

''I'm sure I have no idea. Why do you ask?''

Heat swamped her cheeks. ''Evan's very fond of him.''

"Phyllis and Evan should have adopted a child as soon as they were married. I don't know of another couple who would have made finer parents. Age wouldn't have mattered. Look how they've doted on you."

He was deliberately avoiding any talk of Raul.

"I know. They're wonderful."

"Thank goodness your mother and I had you. I'm going to miss you, honey. Keep in close touch. You're flying home for Thanksgiving?"

"Of course." A wave of tenderness for her father swept over her. "Please take good care of yourself, Daddy. Don't work too hard. I love you."

"Forget about me. It's the piano that's the important thing."

Tears rolled down her cheeks because it was so impossible to talk to him.

They hugged one more time before he walked out to the limo with his suitcase. After she'd waved him off, she dashed back to the room realizing she couldn't go on this way any longer.

The last time she and Raul had been together, it was because he'd made a surprise visit. Now that she'd taken the necessary health precautions and had received her visa, she could venture into his world.

Surely the bush wasn't as inhospitable as he'd made it out to be. He needed to know she would follow him to the ends of the earth. *She had to see him again.*

Reaching for the phone, she called the travel agency that scheduled her itineraries and booked a night flight to New York, followed by two more flights to Buenos Aires, then Formosa in the northeast region of Argentina. From there she would charter a bush plane to take her to Zocheetl.

That gave her about eight hours to prepare. First of all she needed to inform Franz's housekeeper that she'd decided to take a small vacation before arriving in Vienna.

It was after midnight. Since Raul's interlude with Heather three months ago, he'd developed a serious case of insomnia. Lately he dreaded going to bed unless he knew he would fall asleep from exhaustion the second his head hit the pillow.

Tonight he realized that wasn't going to happen. The alternative was to stay in his office and tackle the ever-present mass of paperwork and correspondence.

He opened the last of the day's mail and read the path report on the Toba tribesman sent from Formosa Province Hospital. Another death due to arsenic poisoning from the river!

Furious over a deplorable, ongoing situation, he left his office to find Dr. Avilar, one of two other resident doctors who rotated shifts with him. She was about to go off duty and be relieved by Marcos.

"Elana, could I see you in my office, please?"

"I'll be right there."

Raul nodded to Juan, the efficient nurse who flew in from Formosa three days a week to help staff the tiny government hospital. The rotation system Raul had worked out with several dozen nurses, lab technicians, and kitchen help from Formosa had been working well.

Daily cargo flights brought the mail and much needed blood plasma. Money from private donors who were family friends in Buenos Aires continued to roll in, making it possible for him to have new huts built for the staff, and to replace old equipment the government couldn't or wouldn't cover. All in all, he couldn't complain about the world under his immediate control.

It was a group of men who held themselves above the law Raul wanted to strangle with his bare hands. The criminals owned a mine that dumped hundreds of thousands of tons of toxic pollutants into the Yana Machi river, which fed the Pilcomayo river bordering the chaco of Argentina. Not only fish, but the local tribespeople themselves were becoming victims!

Five minutes later Elana made an appearance. She sat down opposite his desk with a sigh and lit up a cigarette. "What's gotten you so upset?"

"Look at this!" He handed her the path report.

She studied it. "That's the third death in six months from the same cause."

"Exactly." He grimaced. "I called you in to tell you that when the cargo plane arrives first thing in the morning, I'm going to fly to Formosa."

"Raul—" She leaned forward. "You've talked to the Environmental Defense League dozens of times. What good do you think it will accomplish to come forward with another complaint when no one can stop the people at the mine from dumping waste?"

"This time I'm forming an action committee to go straight to the head of our government. We've got documentation a mile long. Perhaps our people can wield enough clout to get some changes made. If you'll cover for me until I get back tomorrow afternoon, I'll take your shift."

"Of course." She drew on her cigarette, watching him through the smoke. "But I have to tell you something, Raul. Speaking as a doctor, you look exhausted. I'm talking gaunt. I bet you've lost ten pounds since you returned from the U.S."

Don't start Elana. "I have no idea."

"Please don't get me wrong." She smiled. "Lean is even more attractive on you. Unfortunately you can't continue to function on two or three hours sleep a night. No man is immortal. Not even you."

Tell me something I'm not already aware of.

"Speaking as a woman, I know a remedy for the kind of tension you're under. Whatever is on your mind needs to be put on hold." There was a significant pause. "Why not come to my hut for the night."

Elana's invitation wasn't unexpected. Not for the first time did he wonder why he'd never felt desire for her. *Dios.* When he thought about Heather, how instantaneous the attraction had been...

The woman seated across from him was Brazilian by birth with blue-black hair and that pale complexion that made her so lovely. He studied her dark eyes, the full red lips, trying to pick out the flaw that had kept the chemistry from working.

"You look at me so strangely," she murmured. "Surely what I feel for you doesn't come as a surprise."

"You don't know what you feel yet, Elana. Your divorce wasn't that long ago."

"Perhaps if we slept together, we would both start to feel more human again."

Raul sat back in the chair. "Going to bed wouldn't solve what is wrong, Elana." *Take it from me.*

Spending a passion-filled night with Heather only to tear himself away from her afterward, had virtually destroyed him. He'd been in a downward spiral ever since. The reports he received about her concert tour through Evan and Phyllis were all that had kept him going. Even then he'd had to be careful not to show undue interest.

"You've never wanted to make love to me, have you," Elana spoke, oblivious to his turmoil. "In fact, you've never brought another woman out here."

He gazed at her through veiled eyes. "Few women can handle the Chaco on a day-to-day basis." Heather probably wouldn't last out here two hours. "You're an exception, Elana."

"But you're not attracted to me." She stubbed out her cigarette. "There's something different about you, Doctor. I've noticed a change since your return from the States. Whoever you met on your trip must be some kind of paragon. I presume she's an American. No doubt blond and blue-eyed.''

She's all that and so much more, Elana, you couldn't possibly imagine. I think I'm going to have to break another rule and fly to Vienna.

He sat forward in his chair. ''Since we're getting so personal, perhaps you'd allow me to say something I hope you'll take the right way. Marcos won't keep asking you out if you continue to classify him in the same category as your ex-husband.''

She had the grace not to argue. ''I'll think about what you said.'' After getting up from the chair she murmured, ''I should hate you, Raul, but I find that I can't. I'll see you sometime tomorrow afternoon. Good luck at EDL.''

''Thank you, Elana.''

The bush plane had gone into a nosedive headed for earth. Heather clutched the armrest of her window seat for dear life. A vast savanna dotted with vegetation rose up to meet her. Anticipating a crash, her eyes closed tightly as her life flashed before her.

Raul her heart cried out.

The bumpy landing came as a total surprise. To her relief she was still alive and the eight-seater plane had remained intact. She opened her eyes to discover they were taxiing over uneven grass toward a compound of wooden structures with a backdrop of native huts farther away.

When the plane came to a full stop, she undid the seat belt and started for the door with her roomy tote bag.

The female pilot flashed her a broad smile. ''You see? You have arrived in Zocheetl in one piece.'' The woman grabbed Heather's suitcase from the bin and preceded her out of the plane. ''The hospital is the largest building with the porch. You will find Dr. Cardenas inside.''

As Heather thanked the pilot, she saw two stout locals, shorter than she was, sprint toward her wearing modern clothing. Feeling light-headed beneath a blistering noonday sun, she marveled at their energy. Every time she tried to take a breath, she thought she was suffocating because the intense heat and humidity were so claustrophobic.

When they reached her, the taller of the two took her suitcase. "You are American movie star?" Both of them gazed at her hair in fascination.

It would have been funny if she weren't feeling sick and desperate to see Raul.

"No. I'm a friend of Dr. Cardenas."

They grinned. "You come to hospital."

She had to hurry to keep up with them. Behind her she heard the plane taking off. Soon she saw a male figure in a lab coat and khakis emerge from one of the huts.

"*Raul?*" she shouted. Gripping the handle of her tote bag, she started running toward him. But upon closer inspection she could see he was a fortyish-looking man who was a few inches shorter than Raul and very Latin in looks. Her disappointment was so great, she felt like bursting into tears.

He made a charming bow before her. "No, but by all the saints in heaven, I wish I were."

He winked. Eyes black as obsidian gave her a thorough appraisal. "I'm Dr. Marcos Ruiz."

Heather stopped to catch her breath. "My name is Heather Sanders. I've flown all the way from Belgium to see Dr. Cardenas. He didn't know I was coming."

The older man rubbed his well-trimmed moustache. "I'm afraid he's not here at the moment." Suddenly the admiring gleam in his eyes changed to concern. "You look like you're ready to pass out. Come with me."

If he hadn't grasped her around the waist to support her, she would have slumped to the ground. Everything transpired in a blur as he helped her to the hut he'd just vacated. The other two followed with her suitcase.

Because of a small window air conditioner, the interior was cooler than she would have expected. It came as a welcome surprise. He urged her to lie down on his couch and put her feet up.

In seconds he was back with bottled juice. "Drink this, Ms. Sanders. Everyone is dehydrated when they first arrive in the bush, and you need the sugar. It takes a few days to acclimatize.''

Heather required no urging. In a few minutes she'd drained the entire bottle. ''Thank you, Dr. Ruiz. I would have collapsed without your help. I still feel so weak.''

''Your strength will come back in increments. Give yourself time. If you've flown all the way from Europe, then you must be exhausted. Just lie there and go to sleep. I'll walk over to the hospital and try to find out what's going on with Raul.''

It was silly, but her eyes filled. ''Thank you. You've been very kind to me.''

''It's a pleasure.'' He studied her for a moment longer, then disappeared out the door with the other men.

The next time she was aware of her surroundings, she glanced at her watch and realized she'd been asleep over two hours.

''Ah. You're awake!'' Dr. Ruiz remarked from the chair where he'd been reading.

Heather sat up and put her legs to the floor. This time she didn't feel quite as shaky.

He grinned. "I can tell you've revived a little."

"Yes, thanks to you."

"I peeled an orange for you." He handed her a plate with the fruit pulled apart. "It will taste good and restore you further."

"Thank you." She ate a few sections. "You're right. It's delicious."

"I'm glad it appeals to you. I'll ask the hospital cook to make you a sandwich when you feel you're ready."

"That sounds good. I plan to pay you for all this."

He chuckled. "That won't be necessary. I'm a doctor. This is what I do."

"My father always says the same thing."

"He's a doctor, too?"

"Yes. An obstetrician." After eating the rest of the orange she asked, "W-were you able to reach Raul?"

"I'm afraid not. Juan said he went to Formosa early this morning and would be back by late afternoon. We expect the plane to arrive anytime now."

"Forgive me for being such a bother. I wanted to surprise him, but it was probably the wrong thing to do."

He smiled. "Instead you surprised Tekoa and Ponga. They've never seen such hair. It gleams white-gold in the sun. You're as gracious as you are beautiful—more beautiful than you can imagine to a man who rarely sets eyes on a woman with Scandinavian coloring and blue eyes like yours."

"I find the beauty of your people every bit as enchanting."

"If you're referring to Raul, then you and the entire female population of Argentina are in agreement."

His comment told her what she already knew—that Raul was no ordinary man.

"Are you hungry for something more fortifying?"

"Not yet, thank you."

The man seated across from her had eyes of black fire and mischief. She supposed all the clichés about South American men were true. They had the ability to make a woman feel beautiful.

"Then I will fix you something else to drink. A delightful concoction, which will in no way inebriate you. Do you trust me?"

"Frankly, no."

"You're an intelligent woman," he murmured. "Please. Indulge me this once. It's a simple fruit drink with just a touch of something extra. I know you will enjoy it, and it will help you to relax."

Did anyone ever say no to him? He was almost as persuasive as Raul. "Very well, Dr. Ruiz. Just this once."

He got to his feet and took the empty plate from her. "At this point, please call me Marcos. I'd like to consider us friends. Understood?" His dark brows lifted.

He was Raul's colleague. Without asking any questions, he'd made her feel comfortable and welcome. "If you'll call me Heather."

"Agreed." He reached for her left hand and lifted it to his lips. Suddenly the door opened.

"What's going on here?" exploded a deep, familiar male voice full of menace.

Heather's head jerked around. Marcos was no less taken back, but he lifted his head with enviable calm before releasing her hand.

"Whatever's going on doesn't warrant such outrage," Marcos remarked smoothly. "Señorita Sanders arrived earlier looking for you. I've only tried to be of help."

Fierce black eyes looked from Marcos to Heather.

"Raul—" She stood up on trembling legs, spreading her hands with unconscious appeal.

"I'll leave you two alone," Marcos muttered, setting the plate on the table.

Heather couldn't understand Raul's attitude, as if he thought he'd walked in on a compromising situation. "I enjoyed meeting you, Marcos. Thank you for helping me."

Marcos nodded, flashed Raul a speaking glance, then left.

The door closed, sealing the two of them in an intimacy Heather both feared and craved. This dichotomy of emotions made her feel dizzy all over again. She didn't know Raul in this mood with his stormy eyes stalking her.

"I never meant to cause trouble between you and Marcos. He couldn't have been nicer to me, so I don't understand what's wrong," she murmured in bewilderment.

Intellectually Raul understood what she was saying, but emotionally he was too far gone to be objective. When he'd entered the hospital moments ago and Elana had told him Heather Sanders had flown in to Zocheetl and was waiting for him, he'd come close to suffering cardiac arrest.

"Would you prefer I be overjoyed at the sight of you practically falling into the arms of a man who was eating you alive with his eyes—in his own private hut?"

She blinked. "But all the men—"

"All the men look at you that way?" he bit out. "You think I don't know that?"

"No, Raul. I was trying to say that all the men here in South America seem to enjoy women more openly. They don't try to hide their feelings the way American men do.

"Marcos thinks the world of you. He was the perfect gentleman and gave me first-aid the minute I stepped off the plane."

For the second time since she'd known him, his face lost color. "What happened to you?"

"I was on the verge of fainting. You weren't here, so he helped me inside and urged me to lie down. Then he plied me with juice and oranges and told me to sleep. I'm indebted to him.''

A shudder rocked his powerful body, but he made no move toward her. ''I don't want to talk about Marcos, Heather.''

She didn't, either. Despite his forbidding expression, he looked so wonderful all she could do was feast her eyes on him.

He must have been up since early morning. His safari shirt had large patches of perspiration and was as creased as his pants. A day's growth of dark beard was noticeable, emphasizing his potent virility. He resembled a dark, magnificent jungle animal, ready to pounce. She swallowed hard.

''Why didn't you let me know you were flying here?'' he demanded in a savage tone. ''I would have met you in Buenos Aires. You could have avoided all this.''

''Because I knew you wouldn't have allowed me to travel any further,'' she fired back in a quiet voice.

His chest heaved. ''There's danger here, Heather. Malaria.'' His voice shook.

"I know. I've been taking the antimalarial pills for weeks now, so you don't have to worry. I've had all my immunizations including yellow fever. Everything's written on my health certificate along with my visa if you want to see them."

"As it so happens, I do. Are they in your luggage?"

She rubbed her damp hands against her hips, unwittingly revealing her vulnerability to his searching gaze. "No. My purse."

"I'd like to look at them now."

"A-all right."

But before she could think, let alone function, he'd found her large tote bag and had produced the desired documents. As he studied them, his brows knit together.

"This first date for the yellow fever—it's right after you flew to Vienna."

"I know. What's wrong?" She moved closer, unable to believe he hadn't reached for her yet.

His dark head reared back. "That means—"

"It means—" she broke in, beseeching him with her eyes "—I was hoping that at some point you would miss me enough to ask me to come to you.'' Her voice wobbled despite all her efforts to sound in control.

"I know we never planned to see each other again, but after you dropped me off at the dorm, I didn't realize—I mean I didn't know how hard it would be to forget what we shared. I thought that if you were having the same trouble, I—I wanted to be ready to fly out at a moment's notice.''

In the next breath he swore a stream of Spanish invective that needed no translation. Unable to sustain his piercing glance, she averted her gaze.

"Please don't be so angry. It's been a very grueling three months for me. The night before last I performed my last concert of the season. With no more deadlines, I decided to give myself a vacation.''

"In the backyard of hell?" His eyes had narrowed to black slits. "Does your father have the slightest clue you're here?''

She'd been waiting for that question and took another fortifying breath. Her slight hesitation caused him to curse again.

"I knew it!" he lashed out in fury.

His crushing rejection of her ignited her anger. "I'm a grown woman and can do what I want!"

"You're *his* little girl, Heather. That night in Evan's kitchen when he sensed my attraction to you, he would have carved me into pieces if he weren't a civilized man."

Shivering because she feared there might be an element of truth in what he was saying she cried, "Can we leave Daddy out of this? You haven't even said h-hello to me, and I've flown thousands of miles to see you." Her voice throbbed from too much pent-up emotion.

His sharp intake of breath sounded like ripping silk. "For your information, you'll be flying right back out tomorrow morning on the cargo plane," came the brutal response. "If I'd realized you were here when I flew in a little while ago, I would have made certain you'd gone back to Formosa today."

Heather refused to think about tomorrow. The only matter of importance was that they were together now and he couldn't send her away. Not yet…This was what she'd been craving.

"Raul?" she implored quietly. "Couldn't we go to your hut now? I never meant to deprive Marcos of his. I'm sure he'd like it back."

An inscrutable expression crossed over his handsome features. After a tension-filled pause, he gathered her purse and suitcase, then held the door open wide for her. Despite his anger, she was so thrilled to finally be in his world, she moved past him with wings on her feet.

CHAPTER FOUR

HEATHER counted five huts including Marcos's. The wooden bungalow-type structures with their own outside generators had been built against random stands of trees, which provided a little shade. They surrounded the hospital, which appeared to be a perfect square and stood in a clearing.

The matted-down wild grass formed a path of sorts. She followed Raul around to a hut at the back of the hospital where a huge generator was running. Nearby stood a pickup truck and several gasoline drums.

She knew something was wrong the second she entered the hut and discovered none of Raul's things inside. It was obviously a guest bungalow, tiny yet spotlessly clean. There were two twin beds with mosquito netting, a dresser, a wooden table and two chairs. Vinyl shutters covered the windows where she noticed a small air-conditioning unit.

He put her things down on one of the beds covered by matching, nondescript white spreads that were probably standard hospital issue. ''This is where Evan stayed the last time he was here. I believe he found it adequate for his needs.''

His seeming disinterest since her arrival had caused the wound he'd inflicted to bleed more profusely.

''There's a closet and bathroom behind that door,'' he went on to explain as if he were the concierge of a hotel instead of the man whose passion had transported her to another world three months ago. That man no longer seemed to exist.

''When you shower, don't get water in your mouth. It's piped from a nearby stream. Don't even think of brushing your teeth with it. There's a supply of bottled water in the cabinet. Use that for all your needs.

''And don't wear any perfume or scented lotion, otherwise you'll be a target for the insect life around here. Wouldn't they just love to bite into that tender skin of yours.''

Though he'd meant to frighten her with his warning, she realized he wasn't as indifferent to her physical presence as he'd wanted her to believe. Under the circumstances, it was something to cherish.

"After you've freshened up, come to the hospital. We have a dining room off the kitchen. You'll eat there."

"Where are you going?" she cried in panic as he started to leave.

Pausing midstride, he looked back over his shoulder. "I'm a doctor, remember? Elana's been on duty since six this morning. I should have relieved her an hour ago."

"Elana?" Through the Dorneys, Heather had learned there were other doctors here, but they'd never talked about one of them being a woman.

"She's our resident OB-GYN."

How old was she? "I-is Marcos her husband?"

His lips twisted unpleasantly, as if he were still harboring feelings against Dr. Ruiz.

"No. As it happens, they're both divorced. I'm going to start up the generator now. You'll feel cooler in a minute." Then he was gone.

Within seconds she heard noise. Soon air was coming out the air-conditioning unit. She ran to the window and peered between the shutters in time to see him stride swiftly around the other side of the hospital in his leather boots, taking her heart with him.

She couldn't believe he hadn't welcomed her into his arms yet. How could he walk off and go on torturing her like this when the mere memory of their night together had the power to take her breath?

Finally alone with him, the hours they'd spent were an endless enchantment. Food appeared miraculously when they felt the urge to eat, but aside from that necessary pastime, they were totally engrossed in each other.

The sun sank below the horizon and the balmy air, scented with exotic fragrances, was like velvet. They turned on music and sauntered out on the patio surrounding the small kidney-shape swimming pool where they swam and danced till far into the night, then made love for hour upon hour.

They'd talked the way lovers do, and had left the world outside their room. Heather lost total track of everything. Nothing mattered but to love and be loved.

But toward morning, Raul's desire for her had seemed endless and she knew without his having to say anything that this precious time together was coming to an end.

When a maid knocked repeatedly on the door, warning them they'd stayed beyond the time they were supposed to check out, Raul groaned and Heather could hardly bear to leave his embrace.

At that point she'd known without his having to say anything that he hadn't wanted their rapture-filled idyll to be over. On their way back to the city, she'd thought she would die from the pain of never seeing him again.

That pain had brought her to Argentina. She had so much love to give him. If only he would allow her to spend some time here and show him what he meant to her, surely it would be impossible for him to let her go.

Heartbroken because he'd left her to her own devices, she moved over to the bed to get her toiletries from the suitcase. After a shower, she would take a little tour of the compound.

Now that she was here she wanted to learn everything she could about his world.

But if she thought a shower would make her feel fresh and dry, she was very much mistaken. The heat combined with the humidity brought out the moisture from her body all over again.

Quickly she dressed in a clean pair of jeans and a short-sleeve cotton blouse. Her hair was still damp from the shampooing she'd given it, so she pulled it back in a ponytail.

Not knowing what could be creeping or crawling in the grass, she decided that if Raul wore boots, she would be wise to put on socks and tennis shoes.

Once she was ready, she realized her stomach was feeling empty. A little food might help to relieve the lethargy she couldn't seem to throw off. Maybe she'd take the little tour after she'd eaten. With that intention she headed for the hospital.

When she opened the door a few minutes later, she found herself in a small lounge with half a dozen chairs. The man at the desk in a white lab coat lifted his head and smiled.

"Buenas tardes, Señorita Sanders. My name is Juan. I'm the nurse on duty. Dr. Cardenas asked me to show you where to go. Come with me, *por favor."*

He opened another door behind him, which led to a hall bisecting the building. As she followed him, she noticed doors lining both sides of the corridor.

The left part housed an examination room, an operating room and a ward for convalescing patients. The right side contained offices, a laundry room, rest room and a kitchen and lounge with a dining-room table.

Heather was impressed that the medical part looked as up-to-date as it did. It couldn't have been like this in the beginning. Raul was probably the sole reason for its existence.

To win the love of such an exceptional man, to be privileged to live with him until they grew old was all she wanted from life. She'd known it from the first night she'd met him, and that conviction had only grown stronger with the passage of time.

She'd seen no sign of Raul yet. The sole occupant of the lounge, also dressed in a white lab coat, looked up from her meal as Juan led Heather inside.

"Dr. Avilar? Meet Ms. Sanders, a friend of Dr. Cardenas." After making the introduction, Juan left them alone.

One look at the sultry-looking black-haired beauty who was probably Raul's age, and Heather's heart plummeted.

Were she and Raul lovers?

It wasn't a question Heather could ask him, but the possibility was already ripping her apart.

The doctor rose to her feet. "How do you do, Ms. Sanders."

"Hello," Heather murmured, impressed that everyone she'd met so far spoke English well. "Ra—Dr. Cardenas told me you're the OB-GYN. I'm very pleased to meet you." The two women shook hands.

"Please—sit down and join me. I'll tell Chico we need another plate. We eat whatever the cook has fixed, so I'm afraid there's no choice. However, you can have tea, coffee, fruit juice or bottled water."

"Fruit juice, please."

"I'll be right back." She disappeared through a swinging door, leaving Heather with serious misgivings for having come to Zocheetl.

If Elana and Raul were in a relationship right now, it would explain his rage at finding Heather on the premises uninvited.

And unwanted?

Raul had never planned to see Heather again. He'd made himself perfectly clear when he'd said a final goodbye to her in front of her dorm. Was it because of Elana?

Heather's unexpected presence would not only have annoyed him for showing up without an invitation, he would have been angered for the other woman's sake.

Was it true? Was the lovely doctor the reason Raul hadn't reached for Heather the second they were alone in Marcos's hut?

While she sat there tortured by her thoughts, Elana returned with a plate of food and a drink for her. Heather thanked the other woman, then helped herself to a napkin and a fork from holders placed in the center of the table.

Her dinner looked like slivers of chicken smothered in rice and beans. It turned out to be quite tasty, but she'd been off her food for weeks and could only eat a portion of the healthy serving.

To make things worse, an awkward silence had ensued. Heather didn't believe the doctor was trying to be deliberately rude to her. It was more a case of Heather feeling the intruder. If it had been Raul's intention to disenchant Heather by leaving her alone with Elana, then he'd succeeded better than he knew.

Feeling distinctly *uncomfortable,* her eyes darted around the sparsely furnished room. Aside from the round plastic table and four chairs, there was one small table that held a stack of books and magazines. Another table had been provided for the TV and VCR. Several dozen videos lay in a basket next to it.

None of the furniture matched, no chair was the same, not even in the reception area. Obviously Raul had been forced to rely on donations with everything coming together piece-meal.

Her overall impression of the hospital and the guest hut was that the interiors lacked color. Everything was functional, but she saw nothing to relieve the monotony of drab walls and flooring. Still, a miracle had happened that there even was a hospital in this oppressive heat so far from civilization.

By now Elana had finished her dinner. She flashed Heather a questioning glance. "You don't like your food?"

"Yes. It's very good, but the antimalarial pills I've been taking seem to keep my stomach upset. Nothing major," she assured the other woman. "The doctor in Vienna told me some people experience mild nausea. I'm still waiting for it to pass."

"If it doesn't, you must let Raul know. He can prescribe another brand of medication."

Heather shook her head. "It's not that important. I'd rather not say anything to him."

Dr. Avilar studied her for an overly long moment before she got up from the table with her empty plate and coffee mug.

"If you'll excuse me, I have a rendezvous with bed. I presume we will see each other tomorrow. Just leave your dishes on the table. Chico will clean up. Good night, Ms. Sanders.''

''Good night.''

The doctor had been perfectly civil to Heather. In fact she couldn't fault Elana for anything she said or did. Yet Heather had never felt more like a pariah in her life. She was glad the other woman had left the lounge.

In all probability Dr. Avilar had been sharing Raul's bed since his return to the bush. Maybe they'd been involved before he'd ever flown to see the Dorneys.

Was that the reason Dr. Ruiz had taken Heather to his own hut first? To spare her and everyone else any undue embarrassment? It made a lot of sense. Just now Elana couldn't get away from Heather fast enough. No doubt she'd hurried off to find Raul so they could decide how to handle a situation that wasn't to anyone's liking.

Heather couldn't bear to think that by intruding on Raul's world like this unannounced, she'd created an uncomfortable disturbance in the rhythm of his life, hurting those closest to him like Elana and poor Marcos who had only been trying to help.

Under the circumstances, how could she possibly be upset with Raul for putting her in the guest hut for the night?

When he'd flown to Salt Lake, he'd developed a craving for her that had been satisfied by a one-night stopover in New York. But that was three months ago. Since then his passion had obviously cooled, and he'd found comfort in another pair of arms, namely Elana's.

Heather hid her face in her hands, realizing she should never have stepped foot on his territory. It was clear that one night of ecstasy hadn't meant the same thing to Raul as it had to her.

Dear God—only a love-crazed child would have followed him out here without a single word of encouragement.

That's what she was. An immature, spoiled little fool who'd begged Raul to make love to her without counting the cost, then didn't want to understand the meaning of ''no.''

Full of shame for her reckless, selfish actions, she left the lounge and dashed out of the hospital, anxious to reach the hut where she could give way to her emotions in private.

To her relief she didn't see anyone on the way back in the semidarkness. When she arrived, she locked the door.

Thankful that she hadn't unpacked, she made certain she would be able to leave the hut at a moment's notice in the morning, then she got ready for bed. The sooner she left Zocheetl, the better.

Lifting the mosquito netting, she lay down on her back on top of the covering, putting one arm beneath her head. Though the air-conditioning had cooled the room somewhat, it couldn't fix the humidity that made the bedding damp. But she didn't care. Her pain was too deep, even for tears.

She stared dry-eyed at the wide plank ceiling until darkness obscured everything. In the stillness she could hear the occasional cry of a bird or wild animal.

Mostly she was aware of the whishing and buzzing of insects outside the hut. Some of them bumped against the small windows built on either side of the door. They had to be large to make that kind of sound. She shivered in place.

When she heard another noise, she assumed it was another huge bug of some sort. But the sound turned out to be a distinct rap on the door.

"Heather?"

At the sound of Raul's voice, she shot straight up on the bed.

"Yes?"

"I hadn't realized you'd already left the hospital. We need to talk."

Those were the words she'd been desperate to hear earlier. But since he'd left her to her own devices, she'd grown up in a hurry. The last thing she needed was to humiliate herself further in front of him.

"If you don't mind, I'm exhausted and half-way asleep. Just knock in the morning when it's time for me to fly out."

"Open the door." He sounded angry.

"I'd rather not, Raul. I'm the one who barged into your world to see it for myself. Now that I have, I'll leave tomorrow and you can forget I ever dropped in. Whether you believe me or not, I won't be making any future visits.''

She started to lie down again when she heard a click. The door opened and closed. Shock made her cry out, ''Why do you bother with locks on the hut doors if you don't intend to honor them?''

''Why didn't you finish your dinner?'' He ignored her question by firing another one. ''Chico showed me your plate.''

Her breath caught. ''I really am a little girl to you, aren't I?''

''I wouldn't care if you were ninety-nine. The bush enervates a person when they first arrive. You're obviously dehydrated. I brought you more juice and want to see you drink it before I go back to the hospital. Otherwise you could be joining my other patients.''

He turned on the lights, then lifted the netting.

Thank heaven she'd had the presence of mind to wear the shortie nightgown she'd purchased for this trip instead of dispensing with sleepwear altogether. As it was, it exposed her arms and legs.

Afraid to look at him, she got up and slid beneath the lightweight cover. After pulling it to her chin, she took the bottle he extended to her.

"I'm sorry you had to worry about me. I promise to drink it."

He didn't move.

Anxious to satisfy him so he would leave, she drained the bottle as fast as she could.

"There." She handed it back to him. As she did so, she happened to look up. He was staring down at her through shuttered lids, making it impossible for her to know what he was really thinking. She almost stopped breathing because he looked so devastatingly male and handsome.

He'd showered and shaved. Beneath his lab coat he was dressed in a cream cotton shirt open at the neck to reveal his bronzed skin and the covering of dark hair on his chest.

Without conscious thought she was transported back to the glorious night they'd spent together loving each other senseless.

Her eyes slid away. "Thank you. I-I'm fine now. Please turn off the lights and go." Her voice shook.

Still he made no move to leave.

"As you've discovered for yourself, the climate is intolerable and there's nothing to do here. This is no place to lead any kind of a life."

There would be no point in arguing with him that Zocheetl wasn't horrible at all. As long as she could have Raul, she could envision herself living out here with him forever.

But he had Elana, and wanted Heather gone from this place for good.

So be it.

Using the words he'd spoken at the outset to discourage her she said, "It *is* a godforsaken place. You spoke the truth. Now if you don't mind, I'm tired."

She lay down with her back facing him and prayed he would leave before she brought more humiliation on herself.

After he'd extinguished the lantern, she heard him draw in a labored breath. "Marcos is covering for me so I can stay with you until you fall asleep. The night can be very unsettling if you've never been out here before."

Hot tears trickled from the corners of her eyes. "Do what you want, Raul. Good night."

She could feel the negative tension radiating from him. There was enough energy to light up the entire settlement. A few seconds later she heard the door open and close, followed by another click.

That's right. Lock me safely away in an ivory tower out of sight and mind.

She turned on her stomach, clutching the pillow to her body.

One thing was certain. She wouldn't be returning to Europe. It was time to go back to Salt Lake and face her father.

He needed to know she didn't want a life on the concert stage. Though she risked ruining their relationship, he had to learn the truth.

She was already prepared to find herself an apartment and get a job. Instead of giving piano lessons, maybe it was time she found work that had nothing to do with music.

If she'd chosen a useful career like medicine, Raul might not have been so eager to get rid of her. But that was something she would never know. As it stood, she had virtually no skills except to cause trouble.

Throughout the endless night she might have slept a little, but it seemed to her as if she'd been awake the whole time. As soon as it was light enough to distinguish the furniture in the hut, she got up to shower and get dressed.

When everything was packed, she made the bed and slipped outside with her purse and suitcase, convinced a different sun lit up the sky of the Argentinian Chaco. The minute it peeped above the horizon, a blanket of heat covered the waking land, smothering everything in its intensity.

Along with birdsong, there were signs of activity coming from the Indian settlement nearby. Children ran around, shouting an incomprehensible language to her ears. It was either Toba-Pilaga, Chaco Pilaga or Guarani. She'd been studying about the various peoples who inhabited this area south of the Pilcomayo river.

Heather had been so fascinated by the little she'd managed to read on the subject, she'd been looking forward to learning everything she could from Raul.

So few people knew about this part of the world, yet Raul had lived out here long enough that he could probably write a book about it, provided he had the time and inclination. How she would love to help him!

The whole situation had captured her imagination several years earlier when she'd heard Evan and Phyllis talk about Raul's experiences in the bush.

To think she was finally here with a thousand questions to ask the expert, yet none of it was meant to be because her ears had already picked up the drone of an engine. It was growing louder. Soon she spotted the plane that would be carrying her back to a world that didn't contain Raul.

As she looked around her one more time, absorbing the strange beauty of this secret spot of earth, her soul seemed to contract in another death gasp more severe than the others.

She tightened her grip on the suitcase and started for the plane in the distance. To make certain she didn't meet up with Raul's colleagues, she bypassed the hospital.

As she drew closer, she caught sight of two men helping unload cartons of supplies. Then she saw Raul's tall figure emerge from the hut next to Marcos's. She feared her heart would thud right out of its cavity when he headed toward her.

For as long as she lived, she would remember this image of him striding through the long grass with the early-morning sun glinting in his black hair, gilding his bronzed complexion.

In boots and khakis, he looked bigger than life, vibrant and powerful. With those piercing black eyes, he was such a fantastic specimen of manhood, she wondered how she'd ever found the temerity to try to win his love.

She smiled up at him. It didn't surprise her that he looked as if he hadn't had any sleep, either. But he and Elana wouldn't have to wait much longer to get back to normal.

"Good morning. I'm ready to go."

"So I see," he murmured in a grave tone, relieving her of her suitcase. "But you haven't had breakfast yet."

"I drank a bottle of water with my antimalarial pill this morning. It's all I want until I get back to Formosa." She walked past him, intent on reaching the plane.

He caught up to her and grasped her upper arm with his free hand. It sent a current of electricity through her body. "You need something to eat, Heather."

She jerked out of his viselike grip and shot him a defiant glance. "Who makes you eat when you're not hungry?"

His muttered curse pleased her so much she said the next thing that came into her mind. "Have no fear, Raul. In a matter of minutes, the pesky American girl who had the horrible crush on you will soon be history."

With those words she ran the rest of the way, passing the surprised pilot before she climbed into the plane. Raul would explain her peculiar behavior to the other man. This was his world. He always took care of everything. No doubt he was slipping some money to the pilot right now for her flight.

Finding a seat left of the aisle where she couldn't see them, she sat down and fastened her seat belt. Soon she heard footsteps.

The pilot nodded to her with an admiring male glance before he continued forward to the cockpit. Raul followed directly behind him and came to stand next to her seat.

She could feel the intensity of his gaze as he stared down at her. "I've put your suitcase on board."

"Thank you."

"Pablo has instructions to escort you to the main airport and see to your comfort."

"That's very kind of both of you."

"Look at me, Heather!" he demanded on what sounded more like a groan.

She lifted her head, steeling herself not to show any emotion. "I'm looking."

The sensuous mouth she'd once kissed to her heart's content had formed into a pencil-thin line. "Are you returning to Vienna?"

"Why do you ask?"

There was a bleakness coming from his eyes she'd never seen before. "When I got into your purse yesterday, I saw that you'd only booked a one-way ticket to Argentina."

Now he knew all her secrets. Another humiliation she would never get over.

"Where I go and how I live my life from here on out has nothing whatsoever to do with you. Does that answer your question?"

"*Heather…*"

Her name sounded as if it had been dragged out of him. She saw his throat working.

Unable to sustain the penetration of his black gaze, she turned her head to stare blindly out the window. "Your patients are waiting for you, Doctor."

He stood there without moving. The warmth from his strong body permeated hers.

She wanted to scream for him to leave.

"One day you'll be asked to make recordings. Rest assured I'll be the first in line to purchase them. Take care," came his ragged whisper. Seconds later he was gone.

She heard the door of the plane being closed. On cue the pilot started up the engine. When the propeller rotated at full speed, he taxied around.

Raul stood in the grass, his face an expressionless mask as the plane picked up speed. He didn't even wave. The moment Heather felt liftoff, she let out the sobs she'd been holding back. As the plane began to gain altitude, she thought her heart would break.

Then suddenly without warning, she heard the engine choke. Alarmed, she clutched the armrests, waiting for it to catch again and resume its normal sound of acceleration.

All she heard was eerie silence broken by the pilot's cry to God before her stomach flew to the ceiling and the ground rose up to meet them as it had done yesterday. But this time a forest of trees loomed ahead rather than a grassy runway.

Heather started to shake and squeezed her eyelids tightly together, aware that she and the pilot were about to meet their Maker.

Raul's image flashed before her. She cried out his name. Then came the crunch of metal and glass before everything went black.

"Ms. Sanders? Can you hear me?"

For some time Heather had been aware of people talking around her, but the woman's voice sounded familiar and brought her fully awake. Her eyelids fluttered open.

"Elana?" she murmured as everything came back to her. There'd been a crash...

"You know me." The beautiful doctor smiled down at her. "That's good."

It wasn't good. It wasn't good at all.

Heather groaned, not wanting to look at the woman who was involved with Raul. She'd never wanted to see Zocheetl again. Now she was a patient in his hospital.

Hot tears ran out the corners of her eyes. "What happened to the pilot? Is he all right?"

"He's in surgery having a piece of metal removed from his forehead. Juan has already informed me he's going to be fine so you don't need to worry."

Heather was relieved to hear that. She tried to sit up. That's when she discovered a cast on her left arm from her wrist to the elbow. She lay flat again.

"Is it a bad break?" she asked in a dull voice.

The other woman shook her head. "A green stick fracture, ever so slight. Some doctors don't even bother with a cast, but Dr. Cardenas insisted. He wasn't about to take any chances where you are concerned. I had no idea you were a concert pianist.''

''It's not important.''

Elana frowned. ''You're a very lucky young woman to have survived the crash with only a minor injury to your arm.''

''The pilot deserves all the praise for keeping the plane level until we hit the trees,'' Heather asserted. ''I'm thankful he's alive and in one piece.''

''Everyone's thankful you both survived. How's the pain in your arm?''

''It's not that bad. Would you mind helping me to sit up, please?''

Elana put a hand on Heather's forehead. ''I want you to rest quietly for a while. When your plane went down, you fainted. Give your system time to deal with the shock.

''In a while you'll be well enough to get up and walk around for a bit.''

Heather was about to argue when Juan came into the examining room. ''Señorita Sanders—'' He beamed. ''Dr. Cardenas has almost finished operating. He asked me to come in and check on you. I know he will be very happy to hear you are awake.''

''Juan?'' Elana interjected. ''I'll inform Dr. Cardenas of her progress. Please stay with our patient and get her to take some broth.''

''Of course.''

''I'll be back in a minute,'' she assured Heather before leaving the room.

He put a straw in the ceramic cup, then held it next to her so she could sip the liquid. ''Please drink some of this, *señorita*. I never again want to see Dr. Cardenas in the state he was in when he climbed up the broken wing and pulled your unconscious body from the plane.''

Heather could just imagine. If anything serious had happened to her, he would have been forced to phone her father and explain why she'd come to Zocheetl in the first place.

With her secret exposed about the night she'd spent with Raul, her father's pain would have been a hundred times worse than it was going to be when she returned to Salt Lake within the next few days and dropped her bombshell.

Since Juan was hovering, she drank all the soup and even ate the crackers.

''Um... I feel so good I'm going to go back to the guest hut.'' She swung her legs to the floor.

Juan looked uncertain. ''I think Dr. Cardenas would prefer you stay here.''

''I'm fine, Juan. But if it will make you feel better, you can help me.''

Not leaving him any choice, she started walking out of the examination room. He hurried around to hold her good arm and they were able to leave the hospital without anyone being witness.

A few minutes later, after extracting a promise that she would lie down and rest, Juan reluctantly went out the door of her hut.

Heather had never broken any bones before, and soon discovered that the cast was a nuisance. Trying to shower without getting it wet required the moves of a contortionist, but somehow she managed..

Knowing Raul would come by at some point to check on her, she'd left the door unlocked. It was a good thing.

No sooner had she slipped on a fresh night-gown and had started to brush her hair, than he suddenly walked in on her without knocking. A soft gasp escaped her throat.

He leaned against the closed door, his complexion almost gray beneath his tan. "I don't remember the last time a bush plane engine failed," he began without preamble. "We can thank God you survived that crash, Heather," he said rather emotionally.

"I already have. Juan said you r-rescued me," she stammered. "Thank you."

A long pause ensued. "Obviously your charm worked on my nurse like it does on every male in sight. He knew better than to let you leave the hospital until I could release you."

Everything she did angered Raul. Poor Juan.

"Please don't be upset with him. He made certain I ate and drank everything before I asked him to help me walk over here. H-how's the pilot?"

"He's resting comfortably. Luckily the metal fragment entered at the hairline so the scar will be negligible."

"I'm so glad."

"So is he. With a wife and five children to feed, he wants to fly planes for a long time to come."

"Of course," she whispered.

"Dios!" He shook his head. "After your ordeal, what are you doing out of bed? You were in a plane accident. It could have taken your life or crippled you so you would never be able to perform again. I want you to get back in bed and stay there until I say you can get up again."

It was when he moved toward her, she saw the sling in his other hand. "Barring anything else unforeseen, if you do exactly as I say for the next six weeks, you should be able to play the piano as brilliantly as ever once the cast comes off."

Heat swept through her because all the time he'd been talking, his bold gaze had been traveling over her body with a thoroughness she'd never been subjected to before. Not even when they'd made love.

Before her legs gave away, she hurried over to the bed where she'd already removed the netting. After getting in, she tried to pull the covers over her with her free hand, but he stopped her.

"No," he muttered in that authoritative tone, tossing the sling aside. "I need to examine you."

"But Dr. Avilar already did that."

His features looked chiseled. "One of the tests came back positive."

Alarm bells went off. "What is it?" At her physical in Vienna three months ago, her doctor had given her a clean bill of health.

"When was the last time you had a period?"

She blinked. "I don't know. Months ago. Whenever I travel, I lose it for a long time. Daddy says it happens to some women when they experience changes in climate, so I've never worried about it."

In a lightning move he sat down on the bed beside her and slid his hand over her stomach. It wasn't the caress of a lover. His was the touch of a physician. When he pressed in a certain spot, it didn't hurt, but it felt hard.

Come to think of it, she didn't feel quite as flat as she used to.

She held her breath. "What's wrong? You look so serious."

His eyes narrowed on her pale features. He felt for her pulse. "Why in the name of heaven did you fly all the way to Argentina when you knew you were pregnant?"

CHAPTER FIVE

PREGNANT—

Surely she hadn't heard him correctly!

"Don't you realize with all the stress you've been under, you could have endangered your baby?"

"I'm not having a baby." She laughed nervously. "Don't be absurd!"

"Heather—Dr. Avilar ran the test twice. Now that I've discovered the proof for myself, I would imagine you're a good nine to ten weeks along."

Beneath his exasperated tone, he looked and sounded tormented. "I understand your fear of not wanting to tell your father, but there's no point in lying to *me* after the fact."

"Raul—" she cried, gripping his hand with her good arm. "I'm not lying!"

His eyes impaled her like lasers before his hand slid away from her stomach with seeming reluctance. ''How could you not be aware of the changes to your body?''

She blinked. ''I'm really pregnant?''

The news had come as such a tremendous shock, she was still trying to take it in.

She was going to have Raul's child!

The revelation was impossible to absorb all at once. That meant she was twelve weeks along, not nine. Counting ahead six months, she could expect their baby to be born in March.

Though she doubted she would ever recover from Raul's rejection of her, the knowledge that a little life they'd created was growing inside her filled her with ineffable joy.

After seeing nothing but a bleak future ahead, she would be able to fly home and prepare for the birth of her baby. No child would be welcomed into the world with more love than she had to give.

While she was marveling over this absolute miracle, Raul was still waiting for an answer.

She sat up higher in the bed. ''If I were regular like most women, and if I hadn't been getting yellow fever shots or taking pills that

I assumed were making me feel nauseated, I imagine I would have suspected it right away.

"But I've been so busy performing, I haven't had time to think about myself. I guess until I couldn't fasten anything around the waist, I wouldn't have figured out I was pregnant."

His sounds of incredulity wounded her.

"You took precautions the night we made love, Raul. Naturally I trusted you. You're the doctor after all. I had no reason to believe that I'd conceived."

He swore in Spanish, making her feel like a naive child who had said the wrong thing. It kindled her indignation.

"Judging by your total silence since your return to Zocheetl, it's apparent you hadn't planned on any consequences, either," she reminded him. "It seems we're one of those couples who defied the odds."

Raul ran both hands through his hair. "Unless—"

"Unless I slept with someone else?" she filled in for him. "Is that what you were going to say?"

At this point she was writhing in pain.

"If you can even think that, then you never knew me, and I certainly never knew you," she whispered in a shaken voice. Tears fell from her eyes. With all her heart, Heather wished she hadn't come to the bush.

Holding her bad arm upright, she swung her legs to the floor and got to her feet, the better to face him. "I'm an O.B.'s daughter. Ever since I can remember, I've heard Daddy tell his patients it was dangerous to take even one painkiller without consulting him first.

"Do you honestly believe that if I'd learned I was pregnant while I was still in Europe, I would have risked injuring the baby by taking shots and pills to come visit a man who wants nothing more to do with me?"

She knew she was sounding on the verge of hysteria, but she couldn't help it.

His face had taken on an ashen hue. "We discussed the reasons why a relationship between us was impossible."

"No, Raul. We didn't discuss anything," she corrected him. "You *told* me we couldn't be together because you would never leave the bush. You also said you would never ask me to give up my music to come and live with you. The only thing you left out was the part about Elana.''

He looked thunderstruck. ''Dr. Avilar is a colleague, nothing more.''

''Am I supposed to believe *that* after you've questioned who the father of my baby is? If I have one regret, it's that the plane crashed so you and Elana had to learn about my condition at the same time I did.

''But there's still something to be salvaged from all this. Since it's what you believe, you can tell her I'm pregnant with another man's child. When she sees that I'm leaving on the next flight out of here, your lives can get back to normal.''

Grasping her shoulders, he forced her to look up at him. ''Listen to me,'' he demanded. ''I've never slept with Elana. If she said something to the contrary, then she's lying.''

He gave her a gentle shake as if to underline his avowal.

Before the plane crash, Heather would have given anything to hear those words. Now suddenly—everything was different.

"Don't blame Elana, Raul. I'm afraid I made a mistake, but none of it matters anymore."

"I beg to differ. You're going to become my wife as soon as it can be arranged. There will be no secrets between us. Do you understand?"

"Wife—" What was he saying?

"You're carrying my child, Heather. I know what I've done. It may not have been planned, but the baby's a living part of you and me. I intend to be your husband so I can care for both of you."

He pulled her into his arms with exquisite tenderness, cupping the back of her head with his hand while he kissed her cheek and temple.

"You've already been through your first trimester without either of us knowing our baby was growing inside of you.

"Dios— I almost lost both of you in that plane crash this morning." His voice shook. He sounded haunted. "I want—need—to look after you from now on. Be assured I'll never let you go again, Heather."

Her pain had reached its zenith. "Yesterday you were so angry I'd come here, you would have sent me right back to town if it had been humanly possible. This morning you couldn't put me on that plane fast enough, so don't try to get around me now by telling me you want to do the right thing for me and the baby.

"It won't work, Raul! Either love is there, or it isn't. To marry for any other reason is anathema to me."

She tried to pull out of his arms, but he held her fast.

His expression had grown fierce. "What other emotion but love could have caused me to break every rule and follow you to New York? From the first moment I met you I wanted you for my wife, and you knew it."

By this time they were both out of breath.

She shook her head. "Then why did you treat me so horribly when you saw me yesterday?"

His fingers caressed her heated flesh. "Because I was terrified of your sacrifice, of what I'd caused you to give up. Wanting you for my wife has always been pure selfishness on my part.

"In order to live with myself, I had to try one more time to reject you. I did it for *your* sake, Heather, not mine. Don't you know I would have come after you in another week? The truth is, two days ago I was on the verge of booking a flight to Vienna with the idea of showing up on your doorstep again.

"But that's not necessary now. After learning that one night of lovemaking produced a child, *our* child," his voice shook, "there's no way I'm going to lose you."

Those were the words Heather had been dying to hear.

Hardly able to believe the nightmare was over and her dreams were going to become reality, she pressed wildly against him and raised her head for his kiss.

Like déjà vu, his hungry mouth descended on hers, consuming them in a fiery conflagration that left her weak and trembling in his arms.

"I've missed you so horribly," she confessed when he allowed her to breathe. It was heaven to shower him with all the love she no longer had to repress. This was what she'd been craving for the past three months.

His hands roamed over her back, molding her to him. "We'll fly to Buenos Aires and be married at my aunt and uncle's home by the local priest. There's a small chapel on the estate you'll find charming."

He kissed the side of her neck. "But before we do anything, we need to contact your father."

"I know," came her muffled response against his shoulder.

He moved her out of his arms far enough to look down at her. "Are you afraid he'll try to stop you?"

"No. Daddy wouldn't do that. He's the kind of man who withdraws inside himself when he's sad or disappointed."

Raul sucked in his breath. "When he finds out you're marrying me, there's no doubt he's going to feel anger first and foremost."

"And hurt," she added shakily. "But it won't be anything personal against you, darling!" she rushed to assure him, pressing kisses to his strong jaw. ''I've been daddy's little girl for too long. It wouldn't matter whom I married, or when. The result would be the same.''

The compassion in his dark eyes moved her to tears.

''That's why I'm going to tell him we're expecting a baby. It will be better if he hears all the news at once. While he's coming to terms with it, the knowledge that a grandchild is on the way will give him something wonderful to look forward to.''

Raul's compelling mouth captured hers for another long moment. ''My aunt and uncle will be overjoyed when they learn we're expecting.''

She traced the line of the lips she'd just kissed with her finger. ''So will the Dorneys. Something tells me our baby is going to be doted on.''

His eyes smoldered as he cupped her face in his hands. ''Evan sensed my attraction to you that first night in the study. Our nuptials won't come as any surprise to him. The attraction between us hit with such force and intensity, I still haven't caught my breath, *amorada*.''

''I lost mine when you told me you wanted to take me away to some isolated haven,'' she moaned her confession against his lips. ''I can't wait to belong to you!''

''You won't have to. We'll fly out tomorrow. As soon as we land in Formosa, we'll call Salt Lake and ask everyone to fly down immediately for our wedding. But I'm afraid we won't be able to enjoy a honeymoon for another couple of months.''

Her brilliant blue eyes searched his. ''I don't care about that. All I want is to belong to you. Are you sure you can leave Zocheetl as soon as tomorrow? Won't it put too much of a burden on your colleagues?''

He inhaled sharply. ''I appreciate your concern for them, but this is our wedding we're talking about. It's the most important, sacred event a man and woman share in life. As far as I'm concerned, it can't come fast enough. The others will manage fine without me for a few days. Right now my greatest worry is you.''

She had an idea he was talking about something else besides their wedding. "What do you mean?"

"You and the baby need a good twelve hours sleep. While I announce our news to the others and take care of schedules, I want you to get back in bed and stay there until tomorrow."

"But—"

"Don't ask if you can be with me in my hut tonight, Heather. I would never be able to leave you alone. You don't know it but your body is exhausted from today's trauma. It's all going to hit you soon. Tomorrow there'll be new aches and pains you weren't aware of. That's why it's so vital you rest now.

"I'll send Juan with your dinner in a few minutes. Eat as much as you can. Later I'll look in on you. Hopefully you'll be in a deep sleep. I want your promise that you'll do exactly as I say."

The pleading in his eyes belied his forceful tone. He was worried about her. She loved him for it.

"I promise."

He kissed her long and hard before tearing his mouth away from hers. ''Come on,'' he whispered on a ragged breath. ''Time for bed.''

At his urging, she got in. He gave her another kiss as he pulled the covers over her. ''Keep that arm still.''

Feeling playful, she flashed him a saucy smile. ''You're hovering, Doctor.''

She saw no answering mirth in his eyes. ''I'm afraid that's something you're going to have to get used to.''

He sounded deadly serious. As she was coming to find out, there were many facets to this incredible man who was about to become her husband. Living together night and day until the end of their lives, she would learn them all and revel in the joy of being his wife.

The manager of the fleet of bush planes at the small airport in Formosa treated Raul like visiting royalty. He gave up his office so they could use the phone.

Raul wasted no time in contacting his aunt and uncle. He spoke in rapid Spanish.

Heather's high school Spanish only allowed her to follow a little of the conversation. But by the smile on his handsome face, she didn't need a translator to know their news had been well received.

"My aunt is ecstatic," he murmured against Heather's lips when he'd rung off. "She's going to tell my uncle as soon as she can reach him at his law firm. I'm warning you now— We're going to be wined and dined the second our plane touches down in Buenos Aires this afternoon."

"I can hardly wait to meet them."

"She said the same thing about you. Their château is open to your family and any friends who will be flying in for our nuptials."

Apparently Raul's great-grandmother had come from France. When she married Miguel Cardenas, an aristocrat, he built her a French château so she would feel at home in his country. Over the years it had become a real showplace. Raul had been raised there.

It explained so much about his background and breeding, the outstanding education he'd received, the financial resources that allowed him to do the work he loved in the bush.

As Raul handed her the receiver, she noticed how the light suddenly left his eyes. With a solemn expression he said, "It's your turn to phone your father, Heather. Do you want me to leave you alone?"

"No!" she cried out. "I need you right here."

The talk she should've had with her father years ago had never taken place. Now that it was going to happen, the impact on him would be even more devastating because her whole life, not just her music, was about to head in a totally different direction.

"I'm not going anywhere," Raul assured her in a thick-toned voice, sliding his arm around her shoulders.

Nine in the morning in Formosa meant one in the afternoon in Salt Lake. Heather imagined her father was at his office with a patient, or eating his lunch in the back room.

She punched in the digits of her calling card, then his office number. The receptionist recognized Heather's voice and put her through to her father at once.

"Honey? Thank heaven you phoned! I've been trying to reach you in Vienna since last evening. The housekeeper told me you were off on a small vacation. Where are you?"

She closed her eyes and clutched the receiver more tightly. "Are you alone?"

"Yes. I'm catching up on some charts. What's wrong? You don't sound like yourself."

"I'm fine." Her eyes flicked to Raul's. "In fact I'm so happy I want to shout for joy." Her voice trembled. Raul squeezed her arm.

"You've been asked to play at the Albert Hall in London!"

She groaned. "No, Daddy. It's nothing to do with my music. I'm going to be married."

After a long silence, "You're *what?*"

"I know this news has shocked you," she rushed on. "R-Raul Cardenas proposed to me yesterday," she stammered. "Three months ago he visited me in New York. We talked about marriage then. After I finished my last performance in Brussels, I flew to Zocheetl to be with him, and now it's all settled.

"We're on our way to Buenos Aires right now where we'll be married on his aunt and uncle's estate. His family priest, Father Domingo, is granting us a special favor by marrying us at such short notice. Daddy—I want you to fly here as soon as possible so you can walk me down the aisle. I couldn't go through with this without you."

She heard him take a shuddering breath. "I'm absolutely dumbfounded, Heather." The pain in his voice brought tears to her eyes. "Apart from all the reasons why this is impossible, you hardly know the man."

"Daddy—" She broke in before he could say anything else. "We're expecting a child in March."

"Good Lord."

She swallowed hard. "Will you come? Please? Raul's going to phone Evan and Phyllis as soon as I hang up. He wants them to witness the ceremony, too. You could fly down together. Raul's aunt and uncle are insisting you stay at their home.

"You'll be able to reach us at the Château Alarcon in Buenos Aires by midafternoon. Here's the number." She read it off the business card Raul had pulled from his wallet for her.

"Daddy?" she called to him because everything had gone quiet on his end. "I love you," she whispered. "There's so much I have to tell you, but it will have to wait until I can call you after we reach our destination."

She had to wait a long time before she heard him murmur, "I love you, too." Then he clicked off.

"Oh, Raul—I've really hurt him."

The receiver slipped from her hands. In the next instance he crushed her in his arms. She burrowed into him and clung until her sobs began to subside.

Still holding her, he phoned Evan. After telling him the news, they conversed at some length, then Raul hung up the receiver. Heather lifted a tear-ravaged face to him.

"Evan's calling Phyllis. They're going to go over to your father's office. If he's not there, they'll head for your house. He told me to tell

you not to worry, that this day had to come
and they would be there for your father.''

"Thank goodness for them.''

Raul nodded. "He sent his congratulations,
and assured me they'll do everything in their
power to fly out tomorrow.''

She wiped her eyes. "At least that's done.''

He lowered his mouth to hers. After a long,
hard kiss he said, "I know you need to call
Franz and tell him what's happened, but we
don't have a lot of time to get to the main
airport for our flight to Buenos Aires.''

They both got to their feet. With their arms
still around each other, she looked up at him.
"It's just as well. This news is going to upset
him. I need time to think about how I'll ap-
proach him. It shouldn't have to be this difficult, you know?'' Her voice trembled.

He smoothed a tendril of white-gold silk
away from her forehead. "Your talent is so
remarkable, your father and teacher want you
to share it with the world.''

"I'm a woman first, Raul. Marriage to you
is the most important thing in my life. I found

that out during those ghastly three months of separation.''

''Tell me about it,'' he muttered huskily. ''But don't forget your music has brought joy to thousands of people.''

''Maybe,'' she whispered, ''but I'm holding my joy right here in my arms.''

''*Heather,*'' he moaned her name against her lips until they were once again devouring each other. She clung to him, needing this closeness like she needed air to breathe. But the precious time with him didn't last long.

The moment she and Raul arrived at the airport in Buenos Aires, his aunt and uncle were there in a limousine to meet them. Though his patrician-looking uncle named Ramon was a more austere type of gentleman, it was clear from the outset that he and his charming wife adored their nephew.

Highly sophisticated, they spoke excellent English in front of Heather. Because she was pregnant and had so recently survived a plane crash, they insisted she sit back and let them wait on her.

The second they reached the château, Señora Cardenas installed Heather in one of the sumptuous guest bedrooms. His aunt proceeded to inform her that Raul would be staying in his own suite of rooms in another wing until they were married. This was a time for spiritual preparation.

Though Heather groaned at the prospect of spending two more nights without him, she was touched by the fact that his aunt held to traditional values, yet didn't condemn them for anticipating their vows.

Heather's parents had raised her the same way. She'd always imagined consummating her love after the ceremony. But nothing about the situation with Raul could be classified as normal or ordinary. Her feelings for him had been so profound, she'd functioned solely on her emotions.

Raul's aunt expressed the hope that Heather would allow her to be a proper grandmother when the time came.

A wave of affection for the woman who'd mothered Raul from an early age swept over

Heather. "There's nothing I would love more, *señora.*"

"Call me Teresa." She leaned over to kiss Heather on both cheeks, cementing their friendship.

Later that night, after she and Raul had met with the priest who would be marrying them, Raul's uncle came to visit her in the sitting room adjoining her suite.

He sat down beside her on the silk damask love seat. "I wanted to see you alone for a moment. I have something for you that I think you'll want."

She couldn't imagine what he was talking about until he pulled a man's gold ring from his pocket.

"This was Raul's father's wedding ring. I've kept it since his death in the hope that one day the woman Raul chose for his bride would give it to my nephew on his wedding day."

There was a pause. "My brother and his wife were very happy. I can see that you make Raul very happy, too."

Inexpressibly moved by the gesture, Heather realized that a loving heart beat inside this man who seemed so aloof on the exterior. She took the ring from him. Having to clear her throat she said, "Raul told me you and his father were very close."

The older man's eyes dimmed with tears. "That's true. Though we were only two years apart, he was my little brother. When he and his wife died in the earthquake, I was frightened because I didn't know how to be a father."

Such an admission was a revelation to Heather. She grasped his hand and squeezed it. "You raised a wonderful son," she whispered. "He loves you, and is totally devoted. Now I know why." She leaned over and kissed his cheek. "Thank you for this priceless gift."

He patted her good arm before leaving the sitting room.

After a late breakfast the next morning, Teresa planned to take her shopping while Raul drove to the airport to pick up the Dorneys and her father.

Raul took her aside. "I need to talk to him alone, Heather. He deserves that much from me. Because I didn't get the opportunity to ask for your hand, it's important he understands my feelings where you're concerned.''

Heather had learned enough about her husband-to-be to know this initial meeting between the two men was vital. No matter how hurt her father was right now, he would respect Raul much more for being forthright with him.

Later in the day, when Teresa and an anxious Heather returned from the city with their purchases, her father was standing in the rose garden with Raul. The way their heads were bent, it looked like they were deep in the throes of serious conversation.

Raul looked up first, sober-faced. But his dark eyes flashed her a private message of greeting that turned her heart over before he went around to assist his aunt from the limousine.

As her father started toward Heather, his solemn countenance did little to reassure her. Deep in the secret part of her, she worried that their meeting hadn't gone very well.

Nervous, yet thrilled to see him, she ran into his arms, loving him more than ever for the effort he was making to accept the situation.

"Daddy—" she whispered. "Thank you for coming. I'm so sorry to have hurt you like this. But you have no idea how thankful I am that you're here!"

"I'm even more thankful you're alive!" he said emotionally. "It's a good thing I didn't know about the plane crash or your fracture until your husband-to-be took me aside. Little did I realize the next reunion with my daughter would be under such incredible circum-stances."

"Please give Raul a chance."

"I thought I was. I'm very much aware he's an extraordinary man."

She nodded, then whispered in his ear, "I love him so much, you can't possibly imag-ine."

"Actually I can," he whispered back. "For you to do what you've done is irrefutable proof." She winced. "Love needs to be strong like yours to make a marriage work. Especially with a baby on the way."

She knew it was all he could do not to chas-tise her for her impetuosity.

"If I can make Raul as happy as Mom made you, then I won't ask for anything more out of life."

"Your fiancé's a very lucky man," was all he said before kissing her forehead. "Let's go inside. Evan and Phyllis are thrilled over your news. They've progressed beyond the wedding phase and are already making plans to fly down after the baby arrives."

Those words meant a great deal to her. But she knew her father was holding back a lot of things. More than ever she wondered what had really gone on between him and Raul.

Later that evening, after an intimate dinner with the family priest in attendance, Raul walked her to her room, but he didn't come inside.

"Don't go yet, darling," she cried. "Hold me. Tell me what you and Daddy talked about. I've been longing to know how you two got on."

Raul's eyes played over her face. "He talked about his concerns, and I did my best to reassure him. We reached an understanding, so I don't want you to worry. Certainly the one thing we both agreed upon is our love for you.''

Heather had been listening with her heart. Raul wasn't telling her everything.

''Raul—''

''This is it, *amorada*.'' He covered her face with kisses. ''I won't see you until tomorrow morning when you enter the chapel to become my bride. This night is going to be endless.''

His parting kiss aroused her until she was almost delirious with the pain of wanting him. On a groan, he finally wrenched his lips from hers and walked swiftly away without looking back. It took all she possessed not to run after him and ask him why he was being so elusive.

With a growing sense of unease she prepared for bed. Not in the least tired, she spent a good portion of the night memorizing her part of the ceremony as a way to combat her longing for Raul.

Toward dawn she finally slept and wasn't awakened until 8:00 a.m. when Phyllis entered with the maid who brought breakfast for both of them.

After they'd eaten another maid arrived carrying the knee-length white lace dress and matching shoes Teresa had picked out for her. A third member of the staff came to arrange the shoulder-length mantilla over her golden hair.

With so much help in getting dressed, she had little to do but continue to talk nonstop to Phyllis about Raul, and anticipate the moment she saw her husband-to-be at their ceremony.

As soon as Teresa presented Heather with a bouquet of gardenias and kissed her once more, it was time to meet her father in the foyer. Always proud of him, he looked particularly attractive in a new gray suit she hadn't seen before.

Folding her good arm under his, he escorted her from the château, through the formal gardens to the front of the lovely little church. The balmy morning was everything Heather could have asked for.

''You look beautiful, just like your mother.'' His voice caught. ''I can't blame Raul for wanting to claim you as his own.'' Her father said the right words, but he sounded subdued and it weighed on her. "Be happy, honey."

"That's the one thing you'll never have to worry about."

When they entered the exquisite chapel, she was surprised to see a crowd of Raul's extended family and friends assembled to witness the ceremony. Once again she marveled over his aunt's ability to arrange everything for their wedding on a moment's notice.

Raul stood waiting for her, tall and resplendent in a formal midnight-blue suit with two gardenias pinned to his lapel. Beneath shuttered lids his eyes blazed like dark fires, making her cheeks go hot.

He couldn't look at her that way if things weren't all right, could he? Everything had to be all right. *It had to be.*

When her father walked her down the aisle, Heather was so excited, her heart danced crazily in her breast. As she let go of him to face the man she loved more than life itself, she wondered if it would ever resume its natural beat.

The raisin-dark eyes of Father Domingo smiled at her, then he began the ceremony in Spanish for the benefit of the guests. Before long he nodded to her, signaling that this was the moment to begin the exchange of vows in English.

Phyllis stepped forward to take the bouquet, then sat down again.

Taking a deep breath, Heather reached for Raul's left hand with the hand of her injured arm. Using her right hand, she slid the priceless treasure Ramon had given her onto his ring finger.

The second Raul saw the gold band, he must have recognized it because his eyes clouded over. Their gazes fused.

In a clear voice she began, ''With this ring, I, Heather Sanders, take you, Raul Cardenas, to be my husband.''

When she finished her vows Raul stared at her for an endless moment, then slowly reached in his pocket. A soft gasp escaped her throat when she caught sight of a large, dazzling blue sapphire solitaire.

Taking hold of her hand below the cast, he slid the ring of yellow gold onto her third finger.

"With this ring, I, Raul Cardenas, take you, Heather Sanders, to be my wife."

CHAPTER SIX

"DARLING? Why are we going this way?"

After hugging her choked-up father one last time, she and Raul had changed into their bush clothes and had left the wedding reception in the chauffeur-driven limousine. But she was puzzled to discover they were mired in the early-afternoon traffic of downtown Buenos Aires. She thought of course Raul had instructed the driver to head straight for the airport.

A bronzed hand slid to her thigh and remained there, squeezing gently. "You'll find out in good time," he murmured, sounding unusually mysterious.

Before long their limo pulled up in front of a modern high-rise. As Raul helped her out of the back seat, her heart started to thud with almost painful intensity. Just a few days ago he'd indicated they couldn't go on a honeymoon for several months. But obviously he'd been teasing her.

She'd meant it when she'd told him she didn't mind putting off a vacation until later in the year. But knowing that all along he'd been planning this surprise for her, she was thrilled in ways she couldn't begin to describe.

"What about our luggage?"

"It's been taken care of. Shall we go?"

Sliding a possessive arm around her waist, he ushered her toward the entrance. It wasn't until they were inside the building that she realized her mistake.

"I thought this was a hotel!"

In the elevator, his penetrating black eyes played over her flushed features with heart-stopping thoroughness. "No. It's my retreat when I come to Buenos Aires for a break from the hospital."

Heather had no idea. She imagined he stayed with his aunt and uncle when he took time off from Zocheetl. But the more she thought about it, the more she realized a fiercely independent man like Raul would require his own place.

There was so much to learn about him. Now that she was his wife, she had the luxury of getting to know him over a lifetime and would relish every moment.

The second the elevator stopped and the doors opened, he surprised her once more by picking her up in his arms.

"This is one tradition I've longed to try out on my new bride," he whispered against her lips before crushing her mouth beneath his. The next thing she knew, he'd carried her down the hall and over the threshold of a door that he'd unlocked.

"Welcome home, Mrs. Cardenas."

Heather supposed he used the word "home" whether he was here or in Zocheetl. She didn't give it any more thought as he carried her through his elegantly furnished penthouse condo.

When he showed her the master bedroom where her suitcases had been placed, she thought of course it had been his destination because he couldn't wait to make love to her. But it seemed he was intent on showing her around his apartment first.

No matter where he took her—from the two other bedrooms to the modern kitchen, formal dining room and study—she could look out over the city of Buenos Aires.

"The view from up here is breathtaking!"

Yet she much preferred feasting her eyes on her gorgeous new husband. Everything about him thrilled her. She would never be able to get enough of him.

"I'm glad you find it appealing. Let's hope you like the wedding present I've got for you in the living room. I've saved it until last."

She sensed his air of excitement and couldn't imagine what it would be. Not until they reached the living room where among the traditional furnishings she caught sight of a black Steinway concert grand piano.

As he carried her toward it and sat her down on the upholstered piano bench, all the joy of the wedding day went out of her.

Since they'd said their vows, his sensuous kisses along the back of her neck had sent rivers of ecstasy through her body in anticipation of their wedding night in the Chaco. But right now shock had rendered her numb to physical feeling.

"If you didn't have a cast on your arm, I would ask you to play the Rachmaninoff for me. It looks like I'll have to be patient for a while longer."

Heather's eyes closed tightly. She was thankful her arm had sustained a fracture because she wouldn't have been able to play a note for him, even if she weren't wearing a cast.

This was supposed to be their honeymoon, and he wanted a concert from her?

"Since the piano has been moved from the store, I understand it will have to be tuned again. They'll send over their expert whenever you say. Go ahead and try it out with your good hand while I make a few phone calls in the study."

Now?

On their wedding day?

Bewildered, frightened even by the change in him, she got up from the piano bench to follow him. "If you need to phone someone, then there must be an emergency I'm not aware of. What's wrong, Raul? Tell me!''

His sharp intake of breath resonated throughout the living room. ''I have to get back to Zocheetl before nightfall.''

''I know. I thought that's where we were going when we left your aunt and uncle's. Under the circumstances, I can't understand why you brought me over here. I could have seen your condo another time.''

To her chagrin, he turned to her with an expression that was less than loverlike. ''We've been so involved with family and the wedding, I haven't yet had a chance to get you alone and tell you about my plans.''

He's been elusive with her last night, holding back, just like her father. Was this what he'd been building up to all along? A shudder passed through her body. ''What plans?''

''Now that we're married,'' he began, ''I'm making some major changes in the way things are handled at Zocheetl. Within the week I'm going to hire another doctor so I can be home with you on the weekends.''

There was that word ''home'' again.

"Zocheetl *is* our home."

"No," he murmured. "It's not a place for you and our baby. I've made the decision that you're going to stay here in the condo where my aunt and uncle are close by to keep you company.

"The guests who were at our ceremony are anxious to get to know you and entertain you. The condo has everything you need to give parties. You'll never want for invitations.

"Buenos Aires is a very European city, fabulous to explore. It's noted for its shopping. I'm convinced you'll be as happy and safe here as in New York or Vienna."

Maybe she was having a nightmare.

"Raul—" she cried out in panic, trying to understand him. "Surely you're not serious! Don't you know I couldn't care less where we are or what we do, as long as it's together? Being with you is all that matters to me."

He studied her flushed face through hooded eyes. "When we married, I took a vow to cherish you, protect you. Believe me when I tell you it's best for you to remain in Buenos Aires among the comforts to which you're entitled."

"Best for whom?" she fired at him, too distraught to remain calm. "Certainly not for me! I came to your part of the world to be with you for the rest of our lives. Now that we're married, you tell me we're not going to be living together like any normal couple?"

She was appalled and hurt that he would even consider a long-distance marriage. "I'm your wife, Raul! Not some employee to be dictated to." Her voice shook.

"Exactly. I intend to cherish my wife by making her life as easy as possible."

"How can you stand there and tell me you're going to be leaving me alone five days out of every week without giving me a chance to prove myself in the bush?

"You have no idea how long I've been looking forward to it. Phyllis used to read me your letters. I found myself fascinated by your experiences. During the three months that I was giving concerts, I spent my spare time studying about the Chaco and the Indians you serve. You live an adventure every day of your life. I've dreamed of living it with you!"

His body tautened. ''Be that as it may, you're a concert pianist, Heather. And though you have a cast on your arm now, it will be coming off in another five weeks. Then you'll be able to practice again, *amorada*.''

Her head reared back so the white-gold silk swished across her shoulders. ''I'm not your *amorada*. After what you've just said to me, I'm not sure what I am, but it's definitely not your beloved *esposa*.''

Lines darkened his face. *''Heather—''*

For once the sound of her name on his lips didn't propel her into his arms. He moved to embrace her, but she backed away from him, not only physically, but emotionally. By now her body was shaking with pain.

''I thought we based this marriage on complete honesty. I seem to recall a certain conversation in New York. *No compromise,* you said. *My life's work is in the bush. I'm a possessive man. I'd want you with me every night.*''

His chest heaved. ''I wasn't married to you then, and didn't honestly believe there was the remotest possibility of it. Now that you're mine, I want to do everything in my power to make you happy.''

Her chin lifted. ''How can I make a home for you if you're not here? When I married you, I assumed we were going to be together.''

''You're all the home I want, Heather.''

The room started to spin. ''And what about my needs?'' Her voice rose several decibels. ''I'm not a piece of porcelain to be picked up and admired once in a while when you're in the mood. I'm not a possession. I'm here to share equally in every aspect of our lives together.

''Naturally I realize there's a lot to learn about life in the Chaco, but for you to suggest that we live the better portion of each week apart not only hurts me—it's ludicrous!''

Maybe it was a trick of light, but it appeared to her that his face had lost color. ''I had no right to take you away from your music. Living here, you can still be a concert pianist and an expectant mother.''

She shook her head in agony. This couldn't be happening. Not now. Not after she'd thought every obstacle had been conquered.

"I never wanted to be a concert pianist." The admission poured from her soul. "If I did, I wouldn't be here with you!" At last the truth was out. It was liberating to say it.

A sound of incredulity escaped his lips. "I don't believe you."

"Then don't!" she cried, enraged. "But I'm warning you now—the Steinway is going to sit here unplayed, so you might as well return it for someone else to enjoy. Have you forgotten I won a piano just like it for a prize? It's sitting in my father's house, unplayed as well because that was my choice!"

Anger made her eyes burn like blue flame.

"Why did you marry me, Raul?" she demanded. "It certainly wasn't because you wanted a companion at your side!"

He lunged for her then, grasping her shoulders. "You can say that to me after what we've shared?" His voice rasped.

Her proud chin lifted. "Until a few minutes ago, I was on my way to the Chaco with the man I love. But another man brought me to this condo and he bears little resemblance to the other.

''What was the reason for going through the farce of saying vows when you had no intention of letting me be a real wife to you? There was no point in changing my name if you only wanted me around when you needed a diversion.''

''Don't talk that way, Heather.'' His eyes looked haunted. He started to cup her face so he could kiss her lips quiet.

''Talk what way?'' With her heart thudding in anguish, Heather found the strength to wrench herself free of him. ''I thought we'd settled everything after my plane accident, but I couldn't have been more wrong.''

Her eyes narrowed. ''What's the matter? Have you decided I won't measure up to Elana? No doubt you're afraid I'll embarrass you in front of your colleagues because you have no faith that I can cope with life in the bush.''

''Did I say that?'' he bit out. ''My only desire is to pamper you and our baby so you can continue on with your music.''

''You mean so *you* can carry on a clandestine affair with some woman in Formosa between plane flights,'' she blurted. "It's really true what I heard, isn't it? Most South American men have a wife and children *and* a mistress on the side. Is that why you flew at Marcos? Because you know all's fair?''

He caught her to him once more. "If I were interested in another woman, do you honestly believe I would have bothered to take a wife at this late date in my life?'' He almost hissed the question.

"The only reason you've decided to take a wife is that I'm carrying your son or daughter,'' she replied in a reasonable voice. "Since you're such an honorable man, you didn't have any choice but to chain yourself to a child bride. But don't worry. Chains can be removed.''

"What are you saying?'' His voice grated.

Adrenaline charged her system. "For such an intelligent man, I'm amazed you would have to ask. We had one night in New York. It was unbelievable. But it's over.''

On that note Heather started for the master bedroom where she'd seen a phone by the bed. He blocked her path.

"I think we're having our first quarrel."

"Our *only* quarrel," she amended. Walking around him, she reached her destination. In her handbag was the card with the château's phone number. She found it and picked up the receiver.

"What do you think you're doing?"

She swallowed hard and fought to keep the tears from falling. "I'd rather live with one glorious memory than the ugly ones we're making now. So I'm going to do the only thing I can do. I'm leaving you."

He folded his arms across his broad chest. "You're not going anywhere. Even if you tried, you wouldn't get very far. I have your passport."

His attempt at levity failed. She refused to look at him. "What do you intend to do?" she asked in a dull voice. "Lock me up in here while you're away? I'm beginning to realize you're capable of anything. I would never have believed it," she murmured in deep despair.

"Darling—"

"Don't use that word with me again!"

"Heather—for the love of heaven—"

Her heart was ready to burst from the pain. "Love has nothing to do with your feelings for me. I'm beginning to think that if you hadn't heard me play with the symphony, you wouldn't have had any interest in me at all."

She lifted her head. "I'm right, aren't I? Having a concert pianist for a wife to show off to your friends and family is what drew you to me."

Bitterness rose in her throat. "It's what brought you to Juilliard, though at the time you told me you should never have come, that it was against your better judgment.

"Well, now it's my turn to say those same words back to you. I should never have come to Argentina. Fortunately your uncle is an attorney. Tell him to send the divorce papers to me in Salt Lake and I'll sign them."

A distinct stillness came over him. "There will be no divorce, Heather."

"Fine. I'm still leaving you. After I get to Salt Lake, I'll find an apartment and start giving piano lessons. It will be a good source of income and allow me the luxury of being home with our baby after it's born. When you want to see our child, you're welcome to fly to Salt Lake and visit for as long as you want.''

She started punching the digits.

Suddenly the receiver was taken out of her hand. As he put it back on the hook, he stared down at her with an indecipherable look in his eyes.

''I missed the first three months of your pregnancy. I don't intend to miss any more. If you're this intent on living in Zocheetl, so be it. But for the sake of your health and the baby's, you'll do it on my terms.''

Now the truth was coming out.

Raul hadn't capitulated because he was dying of love for her. It wasn't a case of love on his part and never had been. Nor was he interested in a wedding night. As far as he was concerned, they'd had theirs three months ago.

The only reason he'd relented enough to let her live with him in his precious bush was that she was carrying his child! He'd told her he was a possessive man. She believed him.

No real man like Raul would want his family and friends to learn that their marriage of three hours was already on the rocks. How would he explain to everyone that his pregnant wife had already flown back to the States?

It was a matter of pride, and Raul had it in abundance.

Since she blamed herself for bringing on this impossible situation, she would stay with him until the baby was born. Then she'd make up some excuse in front of the others about being unable to live in the Chaco any longer, and leave for Salt Lake to begin divorce proceedings. But she wasn't about to tell him about that part of her plan. Not yet.

"Our marriage is a farce and we both know it, Raul."

Wounded beyond comprehension because it had taken the threat of her leaving South America for him to cave in, she started to move past him, intent on reaching the bathroom where she could give in to her grief without his knowledge.

But two strong hands caught her around the waist from behind, drawing her against him. He caressed the side of her cheek with his lips. "You're overwrought, Heather. You don't mean the things you're saying. We don't have to leave for the airport for another two hours yet. Let's make the most of our time here.''

His voice held that husky quality she normally had no defense against. But her world had been shattered once too often. This time she feared it couldn't be put back together again.

"Please let go of me, Raul."

"You know you don't want me to, *amorada*."

"Oh, but I do!" Intense pain caused her to whirl around and back out of his arms. She ignored what she imagined was bleakness coming from his eyes.

"Do you know that until I saw the piano and realized everything you've told me up to now has been lies, the need to make love with you was all that consumed me? But no longer.

"In your eyes I'm only good for two things—bed and the concert stage. Right now the thought of your touch is repulsive to me. But surely that shouldn't present a problem for you," she mocked when she could see that his face had closed up.

''Feel free to carry on exactly as you did before you ever met me. I'll never question what you do with other women when you're away from the settlement because I won't be going with you.

''For that matter, you're free to invite any woman you want to this condo. Why not find one who'll play Rachmaninoff for you,'' she added on a bitter note, and had the pleasure of watching his features darken with lines.

She smoothed some hair away from her temple. ''Now—I'd like to change the subject. As long as we still have a few hours, I've decided to do some shopping before we leave for Zocheetl.''

''Shopping?'' He looked and sounded stunned.

''Yes. It's something wives like to do. You mentioned that Buenos Aires is famous for it. Or have you changed your mind?''

He bit out something unintelligible. Good.

''While I'm gone—'' she spoke as if he'd answered her question ''—you can make those vital phone calls.''

He stared at her for an overly long moment. "You don't want me to come with you?"

"Not unless you're crazy about eye shadow and mascara." She reached for her purse, all the time aware of his gaze following her movements as if he'd never seen her before.

"You could do me one favor, however. Phone for a taxi? Tell them to meet me in front in five minutes."

"First you need to eat something."

"I'm still full from our wedding feast."

"You scarcely touched your food."

"Bride's prerogative. The thought of the wedding night with my husband made me too excited to eat. But since I know there's not going to be one, food sounds delicious." She let the sarcasm fly. "Tell the driver to come in ten minutes instead."

A distinct frown marred his handsome features before she disappeared into the bathroom and shut the door, leaning against it as piercing pain disintegrated what was left of her heart.

Like a drowning victim whose life flashed before her, Heather's mind replayed the conversation with her father outside the chapel doors.

Be happy, honey.

That's the one thing you'll never have to worry about, Daddy.

After pulling herself together, she joined Raul in the kitchen and ate what he'd prepared.

"Thank you for the snack."

"My pleasure," he murmured, eyeing her over the rim of his coffee cup.

She'd almost gagged on the roll, but she had a part to play in order to survive. "After I've finished shopping, I'll ask the driver to take me to the airport and meet you in front of the terminal. I know how anxious you are to get back to the hospital. Far be it from me to hold you up."

Unable to bear his company another second, she turned from the counter, anxious to get away from him.

He was right behind her. "I'll go down in the elevator with you."

In another lifetime when she'd believed that he was in love with her, she'd craved the attention and care he'd lavished on her. But their marriage had turned into a disaster. She didn't want that kind of personal attention anymore.

"What time should I meet you at the terminal?"

"Four o'clock."

"I'll see you then."

When he put her in the taxi and leaned inside the window, she made certain it was her cheek and not her mouth he kissed. She could feel the penetration of his inscrutable gaze as the car pulled into the mainstream of traffic.

She'd been in too much pain to stay at the condo. Another second and she might have said unforgivable things that could never be taken back. Shopping had been the only thing she could think of that would allow her privacy and provide something constructive for her to do.

"*Señor?*" She sat forward on the seat. "I know my husband gave you directions for the department store, but could we make another stop first?"

He nodded. "Where do you wish to go?"

After giving him a directive, they were off. Two hours later she emerged from the last shop pleased with all the purchases she'd made using her own money instead of the credit card Raul had given her the day before.

When the taxi eventually reached the busy terminal, Raul was standing outside watching for her. Despite the crowds of people, his tall, masculine frame dressed in fresh khakis made him impossible to miss. He was easily the most attractive man she'd ever met in her life.

Though the heart had gone out of their marriage, she imagined her pulse would always race at the sight of him.

She paid the driver a generous tip before Raul walked over and opened the door for her. His dark eyes wandered over her in sensuous appraisal before switching to a crate pushed up against her legs.

Heather could read his mind. "There are two more boxes in the trunk. We're going to need a cart."

"So I see," came the wry response.

While he summoned a porter to help deal with her purchases, he engaged the driver in a volley of Spanish too rapid for her to follow. The driver's belly laugh as he pulled away from the curb left her in no doubt that whatever Raul had said, it had been at her expense. Probably something like, "You send your wife with the credit card to buy mascara, and look what happens!"

Until he saw his next statement, Raul wouldn't find out she hadn't spent his hard-earned money. Then it would give her great pleasure to tell him she'd drawn from her own funds.

When she'd been given a twenty-five-thousand-dollar check on top of the grand piano for winning the Bacchauer competition, she hadn't yet met her husband. Little did she realize at the time how she would put some of that money to use.

"We'll have to hurry to get these things checked through with the luggage. Let's go." He cupped the elbow of her good arm and ushered her inside the terminal, following after the porter.

By sheer strength of will she managed to make desultory conversation with Raul during their flight to Formosa. He didn't refer to her shopping expedition again until they'd changed planes and he'd enlisted the pilot's help to get everything onboard the bush plane.

Once he'd sat down next to her and strapped them both in, he grasped her good hand in his. She didn't try to pull it away, but she didn't respond to the caress of his thumb against her palm. Instead she continued to look out the window. The pilot had started to taxi the plane.

"How much longer are you going to keep me in suspense?"

"You mean the boxes?"

He kissed the side of her neck. "That and other things," he drawled sensuously.

She supposed he was hoping she was over her tantrum and had brought him back some kind of peace offering.

Nothing could be further from the truth since she'd bought those things for herself to keep busy in the bush. But as she thought about it, a sudden burst of inspiration took over.

"Since you went to all the trouble to buy a wedding present for me, I felt I should reciprocate."

Raul sucked in his breath. "I can hardly wait until we reach Zocheetl."

"I'm afraid you'll have to wait quite a bit longer than that."

"Then you won't mind if I satisfy a craving that has been growing since you left me a few hours ago." His voice grated.

In the next breath he cupped the side of her face, forcing it around so he could kiss her. As the plane soared, Heather submitted to the sensual invasion of his mouth. But inwardly she was grieving because she believed he wasn't in love with her, and she couldn't bear to be used as an outlet for his gratification.

CHAPTER SEVEN

WAS it less than a week ago that a starry-eyed Heather had practically begged Raul to take her to his hut where they could be alone?

What a tragic irony that five days later she'd finally been granted her wish, and now it was the last place she wanted to be.

If she could have gone straight to the guest hut from the plane, she would have. But she'd returned to the bush as Raul's wife and would not embarrass him in public.

Just a few minutes earlier, several families with children had converged on the two of them when they'd stepped off the cargo plane into the twilight. She saw the respect for Raul in their eyes as Tekoa handed him a basket filled with what she imagined was some kind of native fruit or vegetable.

"For your golden mama."

"Word travels fast," Raul mocked sotto voce to a red-faced Heather before he thanked them in Guarani, one of the languages spoken at the settlement.

Heather imitated his words as best she could. But it didn't seem enough, so she stepped forward and ended up shaking hands with all of them.

Their shy smiles touched her heart. One little girl of three or four tried to touch her cast, so Heather bent down to enable her to reach it. Pretty soon two other children, a few years older, came forward and patted it before they ran giggling behind their mothers.

"I don't recall the last time anyone from the outside showed them such spontaneous warmth," Raul whispered against her cheek. "You've made friends for life."

She could tell he was pleased. But the moment was short-lived the second she suggested that the boxes they'd brought on the plane be put in the guest hut.

His expression sobered. "Why not ours?"

Irritated by his preoccupation with her purchases she asked, "Will that be a problem?"

A tension-filled silence stretched between them before his narrowed gaze flicked to

Pango and Tekoa. When he said something in Guarani, they immediately started running toward the plane.

Without another word to her, he put his arm around her shoulders. Together they strolled to his hut like a pair of newlyweds who were totally engrossed in each other. The way he was behaving, no one at Zocheetl would be able to divine the true circumstances of their farcical marriage.

After accompanying her as far as the entrance, he walked around the back to start the generator. Before he returned, the air conditioner began to circulate a refreshing draft of air. Heather tried to imagine what it would be like to live out here without ever cooling off. The thought was too oppressive to contemplate.

Her gaze took immediate inventory of the interior. The only difference she could see between its furnishings and those of the guest hut was the queen-size bed.

She shouldn't have been surprised.

A tall, powerfully built man like her husband needed more room than a twin bed afforded. But it meant he could reach for her at any hour of the night without problem.

Her jaw clenched. She couldn't handle the thought of that right now.

Aware of a terrible thirst, she went into the bathroom and found some bottled water in the cabinet. Draining half of it on the spot, she wandered back in the bedroom to examine the contents of the basket.

"I'd leave those well enough alone."

She lifted her head to see that Raul had come through the door with their suitcases. Two other men followed him inside with an extra set of dresser drawers. Heather waited until they'd gone out again, leaving her alone with her husband who managed to scrutinize her every movement.

"What are they?"

"Manioc tubers, the staple of their diet. It's their housewarming gift for us."

Heather had read about it. "I thought it was called cassava."

"Same thing. This is sweet manioc. The children suck on the roots like candy. Unfortunately there's a parasite in the dirt that clings to them. When ingested, it can be lethal.''

Her hand stilled on the handle of the basket. ''Do you treat a lot of children with parasites?''

He removed the mosquito netting to put their suitcases on the bed. ''Far too many. By the time the parents decide to come to the hospital, it's usually too late. The native populations are dwindling for a variety of reasons.''

She opened her suitcase to unpack. ''Like what?''

''You don't want to know.'' He rearranged the furniture to accommodate the extra dresser.

Tears glazed her eyes. ''What you're doing for these people is beyond wonderful.''

He shook his dark head. ''No, Heather. My motives are purely selfish. I do what I do to rid myself of guilt. It's no more complicated than that.''

Needing to keep busy so she wouldn't let her love for him blind her to the fact that he wasn't in love with her, she filled the drawers with her clothes, then hung her blouses in the closet.

There were dimensions to the man she'd married that separated him from other men. It was one thing to recognize greatness on an intellectual level, but quite another to see that greatness in action. Truthfully she was in awe of him. Their unborn child could have no comprehension of the kind of father he or she had been blessed with.

"Amorada?" he murmured, sliding his hands over her upper arms to her shoulders. "You're not saying anything. Aren't you feeling well?"

His rock-hard warmth had molded to the back of her body in such a sensuous way, she was reduced to a trembling mass of need only he could assuage. But the knowledge that she was here on sufferance because of the baby made it impossible for her to act on that desire.

"To be honest, I'm feeling very much of a fool."

The caressing motion of his hands ceased. "Why is that?"

"When I think how angry I was on Evan's behalf because you hadn't paid him a visit in ten years—and all that time you were here making a difference,'' she whispered tremulously.

Unable to bear his closeness any longer, she slipped from his arms to close her empty suitcase. Startled when he took it from her, she blurted, ''I want to help.''

He put both cases away in the closet. When he came back in the bedroom, his eyes trapped hers. ''All in good time. For now you need to rest.''

Her anger flared. ''I'm not an invalid.''

''No,'' he replied with maddening calm, ''but you *are* pregnant with my child. That means you'll take care of yourself. Short naps in the bush are not only desirable, but they're a requisite for my golden mama.''

Before she could think to deny him, he took her mouth in a long, hard kiss. ''The staff is honoring us with a special dinner,'' he murmured into the profusion of white-gold silk. ''I'll be back in two hours for you. *Dios*—'' His chest heaved. ''I miss you already.'' Then he was gone.

She stared after him. *Please don't say or do those things to me anymore.*

The gestures, the loving, it was all pretense. Raul would be noble and play his part to the end because she was carrying his baby.

But it was indelibly impressed in her memory how he'd stood there and watched her fly away from Zocheetl without so much as a wave goodbye. If there had been no plane accident, she would be back in Salt Lake, unaware she was pregnant until the signs became obvious.

Once the baby was born, common decency would have forced her to send him a letter informing him that he had a son or daughter. Knowing Raul, he would have been on the next plane to see his offspring. But at least by then she would already have made a new life for herself. They would have worked out some sort of visitation.

Why did that plane have to crash?

Drying her eyes with the edge of the bedspread, she found her purse and pulled out a stack of blue aerograms. It was time to write a letter to Franz. Until now she hadn't been ready to face that task.

Her mentor deserved the whole truth. Whatever his reaction, it didn't matter. She'd never wanted to be a concert pianist. In retrospect she could see that if she'd gone on trying to please him and her father, she would have eventually ended up with a nervous breakdown.

Before that could happen, Raul's unexpected entry into her life had not only crystallized her basic wants and needs, pregnancy had stepped in to seal her fate.

With pen in hand, she sat down at the wooden table and began to write.

Dear Franz—I'm sure your housekeeper told you I'd gone on a little vacation. It's true. I did. But that vacation ended up in marriage to Dr. Raul Cardenas.

We were married in Buenos Aires but we live in the Chaco of Argentina at a remote Indian settlement called Zocheetl. I'm expecting Raul's baby in five months and three weeks.

A long time ago I sensed that life on the concert stage wasn't for me. But I didn't know how true that was until I met Raul in June and realized that I needed him like the earth needs the sun. There's no way to explain him to you except to say that he's bigger than life.

Music will always be a great part of mine, but marriage and impending motherhood answers the question of my existence.

One day soon I hope to hear from you. I promise to write back.

All my love to you, Heather.

She sealed the aerogram, then started another one to her father. That led to more for the Dorneys, Raul's aunt and uncle and her agent. By the time she'd finished addressing them, it was time to shower and change for dinner.

Long pants provided protection, which was why they were the only practical, safe mode of dress in the bush. But as this was a special occasion for Raul, and it was such a short distance to the hospital, she decided to don the sundress she'd bought in Buenos Aires.

It was a modest, summery white print on taupe affair that tied at the shoulders and fell loose to the knees. At full-term she'd still be able to wear it around the hut with her white, flat Italian leather sandals.

The cast made mobility more difficult, but she managed to sweep her hair back and secure it with a tortoiseshell clip. This one time she even put a little French perfume behind her ears.

Her only concession to makeup was a pink frost lipstick. In this heat her cheeks didn't need blusher. As for her dark lashes and brows, they were prominent enough on their own.

So far she'd presented a rather pathetic, dilapidated sight around the compound. It was important that she put on her best front tonight before his colleagues to perpetuate the myth that their marriage was solid.

Since she was ready and he hadn't come yet, she gathered the letters and decided to save him a trip by meeting him at the hospital. To her surprise, she discovered an unfamiliar truck with mounted sides around the bed as tall as a man, parked near the hospital.

When she entered the lounge two European men, probably early forties dressed in shirt-sleeves and straw hats, looked up at her as if they'd never seen a woman before. Both were blatant in their stares, but one of them bordered on lust. She shuddered inwardly before heading for the door leading to the hall.

The man who was the most offensive rose to his feet. *"Fräulein?"*

It didn't surprise her to hear German. Many different kinds of people lived in Argentina.

Repulsed as she was, she still turned to him. "It's *Frau.* Frau Cardenas."

"Cardenas?" He looked stunned by the news. "You are the wife of the good doctor?"

There was a difference between being admired and being stripped of your dignity.

"That's right. Have you gentlemen been helped?"

"One of my assistants is inside being treated."

"I'll see what's happening and ask the nurse to inform you of his progress.

Before the loathsome man could detain her further, she hurried through the door into the hall. Raul had just come out of the operating room in his surgical mask and gown.

She'd never seen him dressed like that. For the first time since she'd known him, it was brought home to her in the most graphic of ways that he was a surgeon dedicated to the business of saving lives.

His piercing black gaze took one look at her pale features and he grasped her bare upper arms in a firm grip. The scent of her perfume mingled with the smell of the operating room clinging to him.

"What's wrong?" came his muffled voice. "You look like you've seen a ghost."

She moistened her lips nervously. "I'm fine now."

He jerked off his mask. "Don't lie to me."

"Th-there's a man out there who—"

"Ernst Richter," Raul bit out. "What did he say to you?" He shook her gently in what she knew was an unconscious gesture.

"If he dared touch you—" The rage in her husband's tone combined with the tautness of his hard body led her to believe there was an unpleasant history between him and the other man.

It was up to her to prevent the inevitable confrontation. The last thing she wanted to do was be the cause of trouble on her first night at Zocheetl as Raul's wife.

"No—" She shook her head. "He didn't do anything."

"But he wanted to, and you knew it!" he snarled.

"Raul—" Her haunted blue eyes implored him. "It's all right. I told him I'd send out the nurse to report on his employee's progress."

Before she could think, he swept her into his office. "Wait for me." He kissed her bare shoulder then disappeared, closing the door firmly behind him.

She stood there, unable to move. This time her trembling had more to do with the feel of his lips on her skin than her aversion to the stranger out in the reception room.

It wasn't long before she heard the sound of an engine. Through the window she saw the two men drive away from the hospital. As the truck accelerated, its wheels spun in the deep grass causing it to zigzag until it was out of sight. Soon there was no more noise to break the silence of the evening.

"He won't be bothering you anymore."

Heather spun around in time to watch Raul rid himself of his hospital gown and mask. He tossed them into a basket.

"What was wrong with his assistant?"

"Richter's outfit cuts timber to supply a mill about ten miles from here, but he's been logging trees on Indian land where he doesn't have a permit. The natives defended themselves the only way they could. This time one of his assistants caught a poison dart in the chest."

To Heather, poison darts sounded like something that didn't belong in the real world. "Can they be lethal?"

He nodded. "My patient is suffering paralysis and having difficulty breathing. Before the night is over, he will probably lapse into a coma and die."

It sounded horrible. "Did you remove the dart?"

"Yes. I've done everything I can for him, but the poison had already infiltrated his system before they could get him here."

"What kind is it?"

"Curare. It comes from the large canopy liana plant of the Menispermaceae family. The natives make a crude syrup out of the roots and stems, then dip the tips of their arrows in it."

While her mind was busy contemplating the enormity of knowledge to be learned out here, his eyes made a thorough appraisal of her face and body.

"You look incredibly beautiful. It's no wonder Richter lost it."

If Raul were in love with her, his compliments would mean everything in the world to her.

"Thank you." She averted her eyes. "As there was going to be a small celebration in our honor, I thought I'd better dress up. If you'll tell me where the mail pouch is, I'll add these letters to it."

"Just leave them on my desk. Everyone's waiting for us to join them. Shall we go?" He opened the door for her.

Taking a deep breath, she preceded him into the hall. He put his arm around her waist to escort her the rest of the way. This would impress the others that he was on his honeymoon. But she knew these were only duty displays of affection.

The clapping started the second they entered the lounge. Marcos and Elana along with four other people Heather hadn't met before stood around the table laden with food and champagne. A gaily decorated cake had been placed in the middle for a centerpiece.

"Congratulations," Marcos offered with a broad smile, smiling straight into Heather's eyes as he lifted his glass. "Welcome to our family. We're not only happy for you and Raul, but we're excited about the little one on the way. The entire village is anticipating its arrival."

"That's right," Elana chimed in. "Many babies have been born out here, but this is the good doctor's first son or daughter we're talking about. That makes it a very special occasion, Heather. Get ready to be watched and pampered from here on out."

For several reasons it was a bittersweet moment because Heather had misjudged the relationship between Elana and Raul. Worse, her marriage was in shambles.

"Thank you for going to all this trouble for us," she said quietly. "It's very kind of you."

Raul expressed his gratitude as well before introducing her to more health workers and another cook from town named Eduardo. When they were finally seated, her husband poured fruit juice into her wineglass.

"Sorry, *querida.* No champagne for you until long after our baby makes its arrival."

While the others chuckled, Elana said, "Then you're planning to nurse?"

"Of course."

Raul put an arm around the back of her chair. His lips grazed her hot cheek as he murmured, "That's still a long way off yet. Don't be concerned."

"I'm not," she replied, wondering why he felt obliged to say anything at all.

If he were in love with her, maybe his protective attitude wouldn't make her feel so claustrophobic. She wasn't a child, and soon she'd be a mom. Her pregnant condition wasn't something she wished to discuss in front of everyone at Zocheetl, even if they were doctors.

"This dinner is delicious, Eduardo. Did you marinate these steaks?"

He beamed at her from across the table. "*Sí.* It's a secret recipe. I wanted to prepare a special meal for you."

"Well you certainly succeeded. Maybe one day you'd be willing to share that secret with me."

His dark eyes danced. "You like to cook?"

"I adore it. There was a time when I considered attending a French cooking school so I could become a chef."

Raul grasped her free hand in front of them. "Fortunately for the world, she became a concert pianist instead. You can't imagine how divinely she plays. One day she'll treat you to a concert, and then you'll know what I mean."

Her career was all Raul cared about. It took all the strength she could summon not to pull her hand away.

"I'm an expectant mother now," she declared in an effort to steer the conversation away from her music. But Raul refused to be diverted. By the time they'd finished dessert, everyone had heard about the Bacchauer Competition and her concerts in Europe.

Heather was relieved when a male nurse rushed into the lounge to get Raul. They spoke so swiftly in Spanish she couldn't understand, but there had to be an emergency of some kind because Raul excused himself and hurried out of the room. Marcos followed at a short distance.

That seemed to be the cue for everyone else to disperse. Except for Elana.

Taking advantage of the moment to be alone with her, Heather turned to the other woman. "Tell me something. Is the guest hut used very often?"

"Hardly ever. Why do you ask?"

"Because I'm going to start working on a surprise for Raul." It *was* going to come as a big surprise. She had no idea if he would like it or not. "Do you think that would be all right?"

Elena studied her for a long moment. "Of course."

Relieved to be granted permission, Heather let out the breath she'd been holding. "I'm glad you said that. I'll probably need close to a week. Will you try to keep people away, including Raul?"

A smile crossed over Elana's lovely face. "You can count on me. The last visitor we had out here was Dr. Dorney. I understand he's a good friend of yours as well as Raul's."

"Yes. He and Phyllis are my godparents."

"They're charming people."

"When my mother died, they were there for me. I love them very much."

"You must have known Raul for a long time then."

"I knew *of* him for several years, but we only met recently." The direction of the conversation was making Heather uneasy. "I want to thank you for being so kind to me. Especially after the accident."

Elana cocked her head. "I was prepared not to like you, you know. But there's nothing not to like."

"To be honest, I'm thankful you're here. It will be nice to have another woman to talk to."

Getting to her feet Elana said, "While Raul's busy with patients, let's go back to his office and I'll find you a key to the guest hut. I doubt he'll miss it."

Warmed by Elana's cooperation, Heather followed her out the door and down the hall. Within minutes she had the key in hand.

"If you don't need anything else, I'm going to my hut now."

"I'll leave with you."

Outside the hospital Elana said, "Your husband probably hopes you'll stay in the lounge until he comes for you."

Heather shook her head. "My father's an O.B., just like you."

"Really?"

"Yes. A long time ago I learned never to wait for him."

"You're very wise."

No. If I were, I would never have thrown myself at Raul in the first place.

"Good night, Elana. Thanks again for everything."

"You're welcome. But one word of advice. I'm speaking as your O.B. now. Stay hydrated. Don't overdo it. If you need help, don't hesitate to ask for it."

"I promise. Good night."

They took their leave of each other. The outside lights of the hospital made it possible for her to reach Raul's hut without needing a flashlight.

Once inside, she turned on the lights fueled by the generator to get ready for bed. As soon as her nightgown was on and she'd brushed her teeth, she turned them out and climbed beneath the covers.

There was no telling how soon Raul would join her. It wouldn't do any good to pray she'd be asleep when he finally came in. This was their first night together in Zocheetl as man and wife. Her system was too emotionally charged to relax.

It might have been an hour before she heard sounds outside the hut. Then the door opened.

"Heather?" he called softly to her after closing it.

"What is it?" She tried to make her voice sound drowsy.

"I'm sorry I was so long." He moved around in the dark getting ready for bed.

"It doesn't matter. I grew up in a house where we kept doctor's hours."

Soon she felt the mattress dip. Clutching the sheet against her chest, she moved as close to her side of the bed as possible.

"I would have come sooner, but my patient with the poison dart wound died on me."

Heather groaned into the pillow. "As you told me earlier, by the time he made it to the hospital, the poison had already infiltrated his system. I know how much you wanted to save him, but as Daddy used to tell me, some situations are in God's hands."

After a long silence, "You're right. However there is one thing I can do so no more lives are lost due to Richter's lawlessness.

"At first light I'm leaving for Formosa with the man's body. He will be the proof I need so the authorities will put an injunction on Richter for penetrating land he has no rights to. I might have to be gone several days to make certain the proper officials listen to me.''

His news came as a relief. He would be out of the way while she worked in the guest hut.

''I'm glad you're going to fight for the tribe.'' Her voice shook.

She felt Raul's body turn toward her back. ''It's not your worry, *querida*. I've already talked to Marcos. He'll watch out for you while I'm away. Elana is here if you should have any health problems.''

His need to protect was starting to suffocate her. ''I'll be fine, Raul.''

''What will you do while I'm gone?''

''I can't wait for morning so I can begin work on your wedding present.'' That's how she'd come to view her project.

''Heather—''

''Don't worry,'' she interrupted him, trying to keep the bitterness out of her voice. ''I won't do anything to harm the baby. Be sure my mail goes out, will you?''

"I've already put it in the pouch." After a slight hesitation he asked, "Can I bring you something else from town?"

"No, thank you. I have everything I need." *Except your love.*

In the next instant he moved closer to her, caressing her hip before his hand rested on her stomach where their baby was growing.

"You're developing a little belly," he whispered into her hair.

"One of these days I'll be the shape of a manioc tuber. Now I don't know about you, but I'm beyond exhaustion."

There was a long, tension-filled silence. She felt his hand briefly tighten on her stomach before he removed it and turned away from her.

Good. He'd gotten the message.

But a half hour later, when she could hear the deep, even sounds of breathing and knew he was asleep, she was suffering fresh agony.

This was their wedding night.

If he'd truly been in love with her, he would have found a way to get her to respond to him.

And she'd thought she'd known what pain was…

CHAPTER EIGHT

EVENING fell quickly in the Chaco. The second Raul jumped down from the plane, he headed for the hospital to find Heather. Because of their estrangement, he'd taken several overnight trips since the wedding to give her some space. But during this last one to La Paz, he hadn't been able to concentrate on anything and had returned home a day earlier than planned.

When he discovered she'd already had dinner and had left the dining room, that meant she was probably at the guest hut where she'd been hiding out in an effort to avoid him. The insanity had to stop.

Exiting the hospital, he approached the guest hut in long, swift strides. Up close he could smell paint.

''Golden Mama not here.''

Raul wheeled around in front of the door to discover Tekoa. His daughter, Vatu, stood next to him, but Raul hardly recognized her. The black hair she'd always worn long had been neatly secured in a ponytail with one of Heather's printed chiffon scarves. Her finger and toenails had pink polish on them.

The sight of his wife's handiwork caused him to expel the breath he'd been holding. "Do you know where she is?" It would be dark soon.

The other man shrugged his shoulders. "She go many places like the bee."

And maybe she was inside. Tekoa was probably lying through his teeth to carry out her wishes.

His vocabulary was definitely expanding under Heather's tutelage. Under normal circumstances Raul would have been amused by his choice of analogy. In a matter of one week she'd managed to win Tekoa's complete loyalty—an astonishing feat. No doubt she'd told him to guard the hut.

Secretly Raul was thrilled she'd been able to cultivate devotion this quickly. It had taken Elana months before the people in the settlement stopped acting as circumspect around her.

"Thanks, Tekoa. I think I'll take a look inside anyway."

The other man shook his head. "Golden Mama say not yet."

"It's all right. The surprise is for me."

Unable to wait any longer to greet his wife and satisfy his curiosity, Raul turned the handle. The door didn't give. Fortunately he had a key.

Excited because he had an idea what she'd been up to, he pulled out his key ring and undid the lock. After flinging the door wide, he crossed over the threshold, then froze while he attempted to recover from the searing pain of his disappointment.

Not only wasn't she inside, but to his disbelief she'd transformed a functional pile of wood slats into a lovely, inviting domicile complete with a varnished floor and paintings on the walls. Matching flowered print bedspreads, lampshades and curtains all tied together by the yellow and white motif of the walls and woodwork presented a charming

French country flavor that rivaled anything to be seen in a contemporary decorating magazine.

"*Jefe* not happy? Tekoa help paint walls and ceiling."

His eyes closed tightly. "I like it very much, Tekoa."

The other man eyed him with his usual directness. "Take too many trips. Miss your Golden Mama. Not good."

He shut the door, then once more turned to his friend who understood a great deal and had always been intuitive. "You're right, Tekoa," he muttered, grim-faced.

Vatu touched Raul's hand. In Guarani she said, "Golden Mama in forest with Pango."

Raul's heart did a violent kick. Though he trusted Pango implicitly, the suggestion that his pregnant wife had left the safety of the settlement for any reason rang an alarm bell. Swine like Richter lurked out there, just waiting for such an opportunity.

"Thank you, Vatu," he answered.

With his adrenaline surging, Raul took off for their hut on a run to get his rifle. But his fears evaporated the second he entered the room and heard the shower running. *Thank God she was back.*

As his gaze wandered around the interior, he checked his steps, marveling at the change a woman wrought in a man's life. Heather's clutter was everywhere.

It was neat clutter. She'd put papers and books in tidy little piles. He'd already planned to have a larger hut built for their expanding family. Seeing all this made him realize it would have to be a great deal bigger. That was one of the many things he wanted to talk to her about.

But first he needed to repair the damage. She required special handling.

Moving over to the table, he caught sight of another stack of papers. A child's footprint had been traced on the top sheet. Puzzled, he looked underneath and discovered more sets of footprints in various shapes and sizes.

Then his glance fell on a letter she'd written. It was still open to his gaze. He picked it up.

Dear Daddy: Since Raul's in Bolivia and isn't expected back for a couple of days,

I thought I'd write you a letter. He's gone to protest the proposal of a dam project that could cause serious problems for the natives living along the river in three different countries. Elana—Dr. Avilar—told me this is his fifth visit in the past couple of months. The process is an uphill battle.

Raul does the work of ten men. That's because there's so much to be done. Every morning I wake up excited to be a part of what is going on out here. Life passes by at such a different pace. Each day is full and seems to melt into the next without my being aware of it.

Oh, Daddy, the children are so adorable. There are too many things I want to give them besides the obvious necessities. I've been making a list. It just keeps growing.

I've already learned a few words in Guarani in exchange for teaching Tekoa and Pango more English. Their pronunciation is excellent because of their musical ear.

With their help—they know what I can touch—I've also started a plant and flower collection. The specimens I've already gathered are now pressed between the pages of books I've stolen from the lounge. The next time I go to town, I'm going to bring back a botanist's tome that lists all the plants and flowers indigenous to Argentina. It ought to be interesting to see how many I can identify out here.

How are you? I'll phone you the next time I fly to town. Don't worry about me. I've never felt better, but I have to admit it will be nice to get rid of this cast. Wearing the sling helps. There's no pain.

I'll enclose some Polaroids I took yesterday. I wrote explanations on the back of them. I have to tell you—if Vatu didn't already have a loving family, I would adopt her.

Daddy, I hope you know how much I love you. I can only pray that one day you'll find it in your heart to forgive me for disappointing you.

All my love, Heather.

Raul hadn't planned to read the whole thing. All he'd been curious about was the person to whom she'd been writing. But the second he'd absorbed the first line she'd penned to her father, he was hooked.

Each sentence revealed depths to this woman he'd known were there. He just hadn't expected to be given insight this soon into the other part of her psyche that wasn't the pianist.

Though enchanted by her inquiring mind, her incredible zest for life, the plea to her father to forgive her for disappointing him twisted something in Raul's gut. He could feel her pain and knew he was the reason for it.

There was a sound coming from the hall, but he reacted too late to Heather's entry into the room. She'd caught him with the letter still in his hand. Her eyes turned a wintry blue.

Dios.

There was a new radiance brought on by her pregnancy. A bloom to her cheeks. The humidity made tiny tendrils of her white-gold hair. Standing there in her nightgown, she looked more beautiful than any woman had the right to look.

"I had no idea you'd returned early." It sounded like an accusation.

"After I arrived in La Paz, I realized I'd rather be with my wife, so I came back. If I hadn't worried about frightening you, I would have joined you in the shower."

Hectic color darkened her already flushed cheeks, but her eyes darted pointedly to the letter. "I realize you see me as Daddy's little girl, but you'll never find what you're looking for in my letter," she began in a frigid voice. "He's been hurt enough. I have no desire to compound his pain by telling him I've made a complete mess of my personal life."

Perspiration broke out on his hairline. Emotionally she was more removed from him than ever. He let the letter drop to the table.

"I didn't mean to pry, Heather."

"Yes, you did," she fired back.

Their exchange reminded him of another one in Evan's study eons ago. But there'd been no chasm separating them then.

"You're right." He took a step toward her, needing to gather her feminine softness against his body and forget the world. *"Mi amor,"* he said huskily before reaching for her.

She backed away from him, stopping him in his tracks. "The bathroom's free for you to shower."

He swallowed hard. "Before I do anything, I thought you should know that I looked at my wedding present a few minutes ago. In Tekoa's defense, he did try to stop me."

"You weren't teasing when you once told me you were an impatient man." The smile curving that gorgeous mouth he hadn't tasted in days didn't reach her eyes. "I must say I'm overwhelmed by your reaction."

The brittleness of her tone, let alone her words, had a paralyzing effect on him. "It must be true what they say about the dangers of marrying a stranger. So far neither of us has come up with a hit for a wedding gift."

He shook his head in total frustration. "You've misunderstood me," he began in a gravelly voice. "What you've done with that hut is nothing short of miraculous."

"A concert grand piano is something of a miracle, too, but it wasn't what I had in mind, either,'' she taunted him. ''At least we can't fault each other's taste. I guess there's something to be said for wanting nothing but the best. However you mustn't worry, Dr. Cardenas.

''None of it was charged to your credit card. No harm done. I'll have it all put back the way it was before. Stripping paint takes a little longer than the actual painting does. Just give me a couple of weeks.''

''I don't want you to touch the hut, Heather. It's perfect.''

''You don't have to placate me, Raul!'' she cried out. ''My biggest problem was believing I could deal with a one-night stand. It's embarrassingly obvious I couldn't. Now we're trapped here with egg on our face while I continue to make every mistake in the book. Why don't we agree that any more surprises just won't work for us.''

''*Madre de Dios,*'' he whispered tormentedly. ''We can't go on like this. It's time to talk.''

She shook her head. ''There's nothing to say.''

"I disagree. Let's go to bed. It will be more comfortable than standing here facing each other like adversaries."

"That's not a solution." Her voice trembled. "Unfortunately it's what brought about my delicate condition in the first place. I don't blame you for that, Raul. I was the one who begged you to make love to me." Her voice throbbed. "But believe me, I've learned from that mistake."

Raul couldn't reach her, not in her state. Deciding to take a less threatening stance, he sat down on one of the chairs. Sitting forward, he asked, "Do you wish you weren't having the baby?"

The cruel question caused Heather to gasp. "How could you ask me something like that?"

"Because I see no signs of the happy mother-to-be," came his deep voice. "You haven't once spoken to me about our child. You show no curiosity about your condition. I haven't heard you talk about the names you've been thinking of, the dreams you have for him or her.

"There was no mention of the baby in the letter to your father, a man who's an O.B. as well as an expectant grandfather. I should imagine he would relish any details you'd be willing to share with him.''

Heather had no idea all this had been bottled up inside of him.

"In Buenos Aires you told me you needed to buy makeup, but I knew that wasn't true because you don't wear any. With your kind of natural beauty, you don't need artifice.''

She smothered a groan.

"On the plane to Formosa you revealed that you'd gotten me a wedding present. I assumed you'd bought out the stores with items for our baby. It disappointed me when you told me I couldn't see everything right away.

"My excitement has been growing ever since. I imagined you'd bought some infant pictures to put on the walls, or maybe you'd purchased a swing or bassinet. Something that had to be put together, thus explaining your need for the men's help.''

Heather didn't want to hear any more. It hurt too much. Her guilt was too great.

"Tonight I found that I couldn't wait any longer to see my present. But when I opened the door, it was apparent your shopping spree hadn't produced one piece of baby furniture. Not even a box of diapers or a receiving blanket."

He searched her eyes. "I'm sorry you thought I didn't approve of your redecorating. Nothing could be further from the truth. It's just that I've been overjoyed at the prospect of becoming a father. I never thought I'd marry, let alone have a family.

"But not everyone reacts the same way to the knowledge that they're about to become a parent. Not every woman—"

"I'm thrilled about the baby—" she blurted before he could finish. "But I'm not quite four months along, a-and there's plenty of time to get things ready," she stammered.

Grave concern broke out on his handsome face. "Heather—are you frightened?"

Frightened?

Yes, she was frightened. It would've been better if she hadn't been an O.B.'s daughter. A little bit of knowledge was a dangerous thing. She didn't want to burden her dad with questions when he had the enormous worry of his patients.

So many times she'd wished her mother were still alive to reassure her. If something was wrong with the baby, Heather couldn't bear to think about it.

"Heather—when I first told you that you were pregnant, I was still reacting to your near-fatal plane crash. I said some things that could have alarmed you."

She took a deep breath. "If you're talking about the danger from the immunizations and antimalarial pills, I've already made up my mind to accept whatever happens as God's will."

But until I'm due, it's easier to pretend I'm not pregnant. I want to think about something else. Anything else.

I want this baby too much. I want it to be perfect.

I want your love, Raul. I'm terrified none of my wants will be realized. I'm ashamed of my fears.

He shook his head. "Let me assure you there won't be any, *querida*. What precautions you took to come to the Chaco represent a minimal risk to the baby. There's no cause for alarm."

"Nevertheless there's a slight one, Raul, and I know my father. I'm sure he's expecting something to go wrong, so I thought it would be better to talk to him about happier things."

"Then you *have* been suffering over it," Raul said in a tortured whisper.

You'll never know how much. Don't make this any harder for me.

"Not really. I made up my mind to be positive and not look back. Like you, I didn't think I would ever get married, o-or have a baby.

"There are thousands of women who will never know what it's like to carry a child. As far as I'm concerned, this pregnancy is a miracle. Especially when you—when—" Her face went hot.

"I know what you're trying to say, *amorada*. Just remember we're in this together."

Only because of that ghastly plane crash.

"Since I'm hardly showing, and it's still easy to move around, I thought this would be a good time to refurbish the huts. They need help."

His mouth curved in a seductive smile that melted her bones. "They do. But I never realized how much help until I saw your creative genius. The staff's not going to believe the transformation."

"Then you really don't mind?"

He stared at her through veiled eyes. "You've turned that guest hut into a thing of beauty. In fact you have so many talents, I stand in awe of them, particularly your ability to befriend everybody. Already Tekoa and Vatu are devoted."

Not like they are to you. The men called him *Jefe.* She loved their name for Raul. Chief. "They are easy to love."

"That's because you've opened your heart to them, and it shows. I'm more proud of you than you can imagine, darling."

Please, Raul. No more compliments. They're not necessary. "Would you mind if I start on this hut for my next project?"

"You can do whatever your heart desires. I only have three requirements. That you use my credit card from here on out and that we sleep on the queen-size bed while we occupy the guest hut. The third one is the most important of all, of course. That you do it slowly and take daily siestas."

Thank you, Raul. Now maybe I'll survive the rest of my pregnancy. "I promise. If it's all right with you, I'd like to fly to Formosa tomorrow for more supplies. I have a color picked out for this room."

"As long as it's the same shade as your eyes."

Don't.

"Blue will be a soothing color for our baby," he added as if he'd worked out a small problem for himself.

"I'll give you one guess what Tekoa thinks we should paint Marco's hut," she said to get off the subject of the baby.

"Red?"

She blinked in surprise. "How did *you* know?"

He smiled. "It was an educated guess. Marcos gave Tekoa a picture of the red sports car he drives in Formosa. It's one of Tekoa's treasures."

"He showed it to me," Heather admitted. "When I asked him if he meant the ceiling should be red, too, he nodded."

"It's a tempting thought," Raul said beneath his breath, but she heard him.

"I'm afraid poor Marcos has suffered enough grief."

"If you're referring to the day you flew in and I found him salivating at the very sight of you, then you're probably right."

Raul had a way of getting back to the personal that disarmed her completely.

"There's one more thing. While I'm in town, is it all right if I buy some sneakers for the children? I was thinking of the kind where these little red lights go on around the edges every time they take a step. The children ought to be delighted with them, and they'll feel good. Poor little Ati still whimpers from stepping in that poisonous manchineel sap."

Raul's exciting chuckle set her pulse racing. "So *that's* what the pile of little footprints is all about."

"You have no idea how long it took me to trace those. They're either the most ticklish children on the planet, or else they thought I was playing a game."

"Go ahead and buy what they need. But be sure to get yourself a pair of them, too."

"Why?"

"Then they'll have the courage to put them on. It seems you've developed quite a following. How did Vatu come by your scarf?"

Heather fought not to smile. "She brought me a flower for my collection."

"You'd better watch out. Every day she'll show up with something else until you have nothing more to give away."

"I'm not worried. I can always start poking around in the closet for some of your things."

His deep laughter followed her into the bathroom where she'd retreated to brush her teeth. "There's something I have to do before I turn in," he called to her. "I'll be back in a little while."

"That's fine." But it wasn't fine at all because she was a woman in love with an extraordinary man who'd been trapped into marriage.

Earlier, when he'd asked her to go to bed with him, she'd said no. Now that he was leaving, she wanted to call him back and beg him to make love to her. Something was wrong with her to consider making the same mistake that had gotten her into this situation in the first place.

Under the circumstances, the day she delivered her baby couldn't come soon enough. Once it arrived, it could conceivably have problems the hospital couldn't handle. Otherwise her father wouldn't have been so quiet on the subject, and Raul wouldn't have purposely reminded her of the dangers, even though he'd tried to play them down.

All the more reason to plan on returning to Salt Lake as soon as she and the baby could travel. Raul would want the best care for their child. Her inevitable separation from him would happen so naturally, no one would be aware it was permanent until long after the fact.

When she finally lifted the netting and climbed into bed, Raul still hadn't returned. He'd only spent three out of the last seven nights in Zocheetl. On those occasions, she'd gone to sleep before he'd come in, and had stayed asleep until after he'd left the hut in the morning.

Tonight would be no different. Once again the tears trickled out of her eyes as her head touched the pillow. At some point she drifted off.

If one of the paintings she'd put up in the guest hut hadn't been the first thing she'd seen propped on a chair when she opened her eyes the next morning, she wouldn't have believed Raul had ever come back to their hut.

When she'd been on her shopping spree in Buenos Aires, to her delight she'd found a Monet landscape painted in his garden at Giverny. It was the one with predominant blues, greens and yellows she particularly loved.

On her way out of the store with her trea-sure, she'd spotted a surrealistic print on the wall called *Sonate,* and had to have it, too. The scene depicted a living room with walls and furniture in lavender, reds, yellows and greens. Beyond the black grand piano, the French doors opened out onto a deep blue sea.

She'd hung it on the wall between the beds so it was the first thing a visitor saw when they entered the guest hut.

Now the same picture was in their hut. A yellow sticky note had been attached to the protective glass.

This reminds me of you. I'm claiming it for myself, amorada.

P.S. I love my wedding present. R.

Heather had no idea that when she came to the Chaco, she would turn into an interior deco-rator. It was amazing how much pleasure she got from choosing colors and fabrics, making everything come alive. Her hobby had kept her so engrossed over the past month and a half, she was close to finishing all the huts.

Alone for the last of her breakfast, she finished her juice, anxious to get back to her work on the one for the cooks. She'd chosen a light sage-green for the walls that she felt was so attractive, she wanted to talk to Raul about doing the hospital lounge in the same color.

As if thinking about her husband had conjured him up, he walked into the dining room still dressed in his surgical gown. He'd been awakened earlier to perform an emergency appendectomy. Her breath grew shallow the second she caught sight of his arresting face. It shocked her that she could still react to him this way when only a few hours ago she'd studied him while he slept.

His black eyes sought hers, but she couldn't read what was in their expression. ''I'm glad you're still here. It saves me sending Tekoa to find you. Come in the examining room.''

As she did his bidding, her pulse started to run away with her.

''What is it?'' She felt a trifle anxious as he closed the door, wondering why he was behaving so mysteriously.

"First let's get you up here." Before she knew it, he'd picked her up and set her on the examining table with the utmost care. It was the first time in six weeks she'd felt his arms go around her. Though it had only lasted a moment, the contact had electrified her body.

He brushed his mouth against hers in an unexpected gesture, sending tendrils of delight unfurling through her system. "How would you like to be free of that cast?"

"Oh, Raul—that would be wonderful!"

His eyes narrowed on her features. "I thought that might bring a smile to your face. Let me help you lie down so you'll be more comfortable."

It was so strange to think they'd been living as man and wife all this time, sleeping in the same bed. Yet there'd been more intimacy between them just now than in all the time she'd been in the bush.

Her love for him had grown so deep, she was afraid he would see it in her eyes and pity her that much more. To hide her emotions, she turned her face toward the wall.

She didn't have to wait long to be rid of her burden. All of a sudden she was relieved of the weight and felt her arm rise a little of its own accord.

"How does that feel?" came the deep voice she adored.

"Almost like I don't have an arm."

He chuckled. "That's a normal reaction."

Her head moved to the other side to make sure her arm was still there. It looked paler where the cast had been, but it felt fine.

"You're as good as new," he said in a thick-toned voice. "But for the next twenty-four hours, ease your way back to normal usage."

"Thank you," she whispered, and started to get up, but he held her shoulder down.

"While I've got you here, might as well give you a checkup and save Elana the trouble."

For the next few minutes, he became the total doctor, checking her vital signs.

"Our baby has a good, strong heartbeat. Everything appears normal. Your measurements are excellent, Mrs. Cardenas." In the next breath, she felt his lips rove over her belly, giving her featherlight kisses. He hadn't had a chance to shave yet. The slight rasp of his beard brushed against her satiny skin, causing her body to leap to pulsating life. She ached for him.

But as he lifted his head, she saw something in his eyes that troubled her. "What's wrong?"

His gaze fused with hers. "If you do everything I tell you, you're going to have a healthy child, *amorada*." He stepped away from her. "Leave a specimen in the rest room, then wait for me in my office."

She blinked. "If there's something you need to tell me, why not here?"

There was the slightest hardening of his features as he paused in the doorway. "Because you're my wife, and I've never seen you looking more desirable. I'm afraid I'm feeling anything but professional at the moment. So I'm going to check on my patient, then meet you across the hall."

Stunned by his admission, she watched him disappear from the room. He'd left in such a hurry, he forgot to help her off the table. She managed without him, but her legs almost buckled in the process, testimony of her weakened state after the sensuous way he'd just kissed her and their baby.

Five minutes later he swept in his office where she was waiting. She moaned because the banked fires she'd glimpsed in his eyes moments ago were no longer in evidence. Maybe she'd just imagined that for a moment he'd wanted her the same way he had back in New York.

"Stay seated, Heather."

"That sounds ominous," she murmured, complying with his wishes as he went around his desk to his swivel chair.

"Nothing so serious. Your blood pressure's up a little. To take care of that, we'll restrict all salt from your diet and you're going to have to stop the remodeling."

"But—"

"There can't be any buts when it's your life and the life of our baby we're talking about. You can still move around and enjoy your hobbies. But I want you to lie down for at least an hour twice a day between breakfast and dinner.''

''The cook's hut is only half finished, and—''

''I'll work on it when I'm not on rotation. You've taught the men what to do. They'll help me. Your job is to relax. By the way, my aunt and uncle have extended us an invitation for next weekend. It's Uncle Ramon's birthday.''

Heather had the impression he was holding something back. The mention of his family disconcerted her. She looked down at her hands, preferring to stay in Zocheetl where Raul's work separated them for long periods each day. That made it easier to keep up a happy front around the staff. Forced to pretend in front of Teresa and Ramon for two or three days nonstop would be a different story altogether.

For her own self-preservation, she didn't dare fly to Buenos Aires with him. The temptation to throw herself at him would be too great. She would end up despising herself more than she already did.

"Obviously the idea holds little appeal."

"It isn't that. They're wonderful people and I'd love to see them again. It's just that I don't feel like traveling right now."

She knew it was a feeble excuse. So did he. Up until this moment she'd shown no reluctance to get on a plane to buy more supplies in Formosa.

The intensity of his dark gaze seemed to reach into her soul. "I'll make up a legitimate excuse why we can't come."

"Don't let me stop you from going!" she urged him, assailed by guilt.

"Until our baby is born, I have no intention of leaving your side."

She got up from the chair. "I—I need to use the rest room again." It was another excuse he could see right through, but she had to get away from him before she broke down in front of him.

As she dashed from the room, she thought she heard him call her name. But it didn't matter. There wasn't anything more to say. Nothing could be done about their wretched situation until the baby made its presence known in the world.

I bet you're counting the hours until the noose is no longer around your neck. I don't blame you, my darling. As soon as it's possible, I'll give you your freedom. I swear it.

CHAPTER NINE

"GOLDEN Mama?"

"What is it, Tekoa?"

He'd run into the hospital kitchen where she was baking a cake for Marcos. Raul had pronounced her bone fully healed. It was liberating to have the use of her arm again, and couldn't have come at a better time. Tonight they were going to throw the esteemed doctor a surprise birthday party.

"Come quick! Plane here."

"Just a minute."

She made sure the oven was up to temperature, then she put the cake inside.

"I'll watch the time," Chico volunteered. He was busy preparing lunch for everyone.

"Thanks. I'll be right back."

She followed Tekoa out the rear exit behind the kitchen.

"*Jefe* gone. You say what to do."

Heather wasn't the only one who wished the *Jefe* hadn't driven to the mill. He'd left at first light determined to find out if Ernst Richter was obeying the recent court order placed on him.

Since her one and only encounter with the disgusting man, she'd heard horror stories about him. Until Raul returned, she wouldn't be able to breathe normally. He'd promised to be back soon.

She approached the plane where the female pilot who had flown her to Zocheetl the first time was talking to Pango. He kept shaking his head.

"*Buenos Dias, señora.* What seems to be the problem?"

"Dr. Cardenas sent some cargo your workers are afraid of. Come inside and I will show you."

Heather couldn't imagine, but she did the pilot's bidding. To her amazement she saw a piano blocking the aisle. It was an old upright finished in a dark wood that had seen better days.

Raul. He never gave up. This was no coincidence, not when her cast had just come off.

"They helped me undo the padding. But when they heard a noise, they ran off."

Tekoa and Pango stood in the opening looking anxious. "Bad spirit inside, Golden Mama."

Comprehension dawned. They'd never seen a piano before and didn't have a clue what it was. She had to think fast.

"Pango? Is there a bad spirit inside your flute?"

He scratched his head, then pulled the little instrument he'd whittled from his pocket.

"Go on," she encouraged him. "Play it for us."

He lifted it to his lips and played a tune of his own creation, one she'd heard many times.

"That was beautiful. Tekoa? Does his flute have a bad spirit?"

"No, Golden Mama."

"This—" she patted the top of the piano "—has a good spirit."

While they watched in rapt attention, she moved around to the front. The squeeze wouldn't have been as tight if she weren't close to five months along now.

It felt like years instead of months since she'd last looked at a piano keyboard. Some of the ivories were chipped, indicating a lot of use.

Two pairs of dark eyes were riveted on her.

She smiled to herself. "Listen."

With one hand she played the same tune Pango had played on his flute. She did it slowly, key after key.

Their fear began to dissipate. Soon their mouths broke into smiles and then grins. They drew closer. At this point the pilot was smiling, too.

"Again—" they both said at the same time, like excited children.

"First we have to move the piano off the plane. The pilot has work to do."

"*Gracias,*" she whispered in Heather's ear as the men managed to get the unwieldy instrument onto the grass without damaging it.

Heather answered, "*De nada,*" before climbing out.

Once the pilot taxied around and took off, the men begged her to play. She smiled at Pango. "Get out your flute. We'll do it together."

He put it to his lips and they began a duet. After the fifth rendition, a crowd from the settlement had gathered around. Soon every child and adult had taken a turn pressing the keys. The little ones would jump back giggling.

Their pleasure in the music was a joy to watch. Unable to resist, she started to play some nursery rhymes with one hand. When she joined the other hand and started to jazz it up, the expression in their eyes turned to one of awe.

Oblivious of the grass and the burning noonday sun, she suddenly found herself playing Grieg's Wedding Day at Troldhaugen, a favorite piece of her mother's. Until now she hadn't realized how much she'd missed the piano.

To think this gentle group of Chaco natives was hearing music of the great Norwegian composer for the first time! The wonder of it all filled her with pure delight. When she ended the romantic piece, she actually laughed out loud.

As her voice penetrated the stillness, she heard clapping behind her and spun around.

Her husband stood at the back of the mesmerized group. Even from the distance separating them, his intelligent black eyes held a telltale luster. She thanked providence he'd returned safely.

Raul—

"H-how long have you been standing there?"

"Long enough to know I didn't make a mistake with your wedding present this time."

She couldn't deny the obvious. Wiping the perspiration off her forehead with the back of her hand she said, "Where do you want the piano to go? I'm afraid it will disturb your patients if we put it in the hospital lounge."

His lips curved into that half smile she adored. "It'll be fine there for tonight's party. Tomorrow will be soon enough to take it to the guest hut. After your open air concert, everyone in the settlement will beat a path to your door to hear more. When you're in the mood that is..."

She averted her eyes while he gave instructions to Tekoa and Pango. Everyone followed them to the hospital except her husband who moved inexorably toward her.

He reached for her arm, running his fingers in caressing motions over the skin that hadn't seen the sun for such a long time. Like last week, when he removed the cast, fire shot through her body at the contact.

His eyes captured hers. "How does your arm feel after giving your hand such a workout?"

She couldn't talk, couldn't swallow. She couldn't do anything with him standing this close, touching her, igniting her desire. She wanted him so badly, she felt exquisite pain...

"Fine," she finally managed to whisper.

"Thank goodness," she heard him murmur before his head descended and his mouth covered hers with a refined savagery that set her body trembling.

Maybe it was a combination of the heat and the emotion she was feeling because he'd come to no harm. All she knew was that when he gathered her in his arms, the knowledge that he wasn't in love with her seemed to take a back seat to the passion he'd aroused in her.

His hand roved to her lower back, pressing her as close as was physically possible, but it wasn't close enough for Heather. Not when she was in her second trimester.

"Feel that?" he said in a ragged voice.

She groaned inside. *Don't you know I'm aware of our child every moment of my life?*

"Our baby's right there, *mi amor,* growing bigger every day. I know I have to wait, but I never realized it would be this hard."

His words reminded her not to get too carried away. It was the baby he was living for. Heather was simply the vehicle. "The cake!" she cried, tearing her lips from his.

"What are you talking about?" He fought for her mouth once more, but she managed to ease herself from his powerful arms.

"Marcos's birthday cake. I left it in the oven. It's probably burned!"

"If it has, there's still time to make another one. I'll help."

He let go of her shoulders with seeming reluctance. They started for the hospital. Before they'd gone three feet, he found her hand and kept a firm grasp on it all the way to the kitchen.

Right now it would be so easy to stay in denial, to believe that he'd kissed her because he couldn't help himself. But it wasn't true. The lines were blurred when you felt gratitude to the woman who was going to be the mother of your child.

Before Raul had learned about her pregnancy, he'd been willing to say goodbye forever. His rejection had taught her that physical intimacy didn't automatically mean love forever after. She was living here on borrowed time and would be an utter fool to forget it for even one second.

Elana finally returned to the examining room. ''I apologize for being gone so long, Heather.''

''Was there an emergency?''

''The worst kind.''

''What's wrong?''

"Your husband demanded a detailed report of your physical before he drove off with Pango. He makes a terrible expectant father."

Heather had no idea he hadn't already left. He'd been working on the yearly census of the natives in the area for the better part of a week.

"And you make a terrible tease, Elana. I would never have guessed it when we first met." Surprisingly the two women had become good friends over the past five months.

Five months of living with Raul who treated her like a concerned brother.

There'd been two brief moments of intimacy, but after the delivery of the piano, Raul had only occasionally given her a neck rub, or kissed her cheek coming and going. It had been months since he'd reached for her in bed, if only to feel the baby for a moment.

His acceptance of the status quo offered absolute proof of his disinterest in her. It was hard to believe they had ever shared a passion-filled night of lovemaking.

He wasn't the same man anymore. If he had any idea how shattered she was that he no longer felt desire for her...

Their child's welfare was all that occupied Raul's thoughts these days. Though he would deny it, part of her wondered if he wasn't starting to worry that some abnormality might show up at delivery. It could explain why he'd become so taciturn around the staff.

Speaking of the baby, it must not have liked the exam. Either a tiny arm or leg had started hammering away in the same sore spot. While she sat up, she had to press her hand against it in an effort to counteract the pain.

"Need some help?"

"Thank you, but I'd like to think I can still do this by myself," she muttered, trying to figure out a graceful way to get down off the examining table.

With a couple of grunts and groans she managed to work her way to the edge and step onto the floor without making a complete fool of herself.

"Good for you."

One look at Elana and they both chuckled. "Last week Raul took me in the truck to see a Toba settlement. On the way we spotted a plump little pink fairy armadillo burrowing into an anthill.

"The poor thing was so dragged down by her tail, she could scarcely move. Raul started laughing. I knew he was making comparisons. It was horrible!"

"I wouldn't worry too much. The man never takes his eyes off you."

"I could say the same thing about Marcos where you're concerned, Elana."

"I'm waiting to see how long his interest lasts."

"Well—if it's any consolation, I've been out here five months and in all that time, I've never seen him leave your side if he could help it."

Taking a calculated risk Heather confided, "Raul told me Marcos chose to renew his contract to stay on another year, but that's strictly classified."

"You're telling me the truth?"

For once Heather had caught Elana unaware. It was obvious the news had pleased her. "So, Dr. Avilar—How about some good news for me?"

The other woman cocked her head. "All things considered, you're coming along fine, but the *Jefe* has rendered his edict. No more piano lessons. It's complete bedrest now."

"Is that *only his* opinion, or does my O.B. happen to agree with him?"

To Heather's disappointment, Elana nodded. "You're starting your ninth month. To be on the safe side, it's time to take up a new hobby where you can prop your feet all day to minimize the swelling."

"That doesn't leave me with much I can do."

Elana darted her a shrewd regard. "I can think of one safe activity I haven't seen you working on yet."

Experiencing a stab of guilt, Heather averted her eyes.

"I didn't say that to make you uncomfortable. But for a woman who could win homemaker of the year on two continents, your marked lack of activity in the baby department simply doesn't ring true. Not for you."

Heather's breath caught. "Raul's been taking care of that." Their hut bulged from baby paraphernalia. "Has he been talking to you?"

The other woman's brows lifted. "These days he doesn't say much to anyone."

Her guilt compounded. "Forgive me. I didn't mean to put you on the defensive."

"You didn't."

"Th-things will be different after the baby's born." As soon as Heather returned to the States, Raul's life would get back to normal. She'd only seen him truly happy in New York when he'd given in to his fleeting passion, never dreaming where it would lead.

She patted Elana's arm. "Thank you for everything."

"You're welcome. Before I forget, Raul said something came for you in the mail. He had Tekoa take it to your hut."

"Good." Heather could stand some diversion about now. "I'll see you at dinner."

"Wrong. You'll only see me from now on when I come to visit you."

Heather nodded before leaving the hospital. The walk across the compound took longer than it used to. When she finally entered the hut, she expected to see a large carton standing in the room. Instead a small package had been placed on the table.

Curious, she reached for it and looked at the return address. It was from her father.

Her hands trembled with excitement as she undid the wrapping and lifted the lid. Inside was an adorable white christening outfit and matching bonnet. He'd put a note in the tissue.

This was your christening outfit, Heather. Your mother kept it in the cupboard waiting for the day when she could give it to you for your own baby. That time is almost here. I'm set to fly down at a moment's notice.

Your old dad loves you, honey.

Her father thought everything was fine with her. Yet once again she was living a lie, keeping more secrets from him, from Raul…

She dropped the note before collapsing on the bed in a paroxysm of tears. Deep heaving sobs shook her body. For weeks she'd been holding back, but her father's gift had opened the floodgates.

"*Dios,* Heather—"

At the sound of Raul's voice, she let out a pained gasp. She hadn't heard the truck return, and wanted to die at being caught like this.

Hastily wiping her eyes she cried, "W-what are you doing b-back so soon?"

"I had a feeling you might need me."

He was hovering again.

"I'm fine. You should be out there finishing up the census." For every head of family listed, the government provided funding for the hospital. It was little wonder Raul had to rely on private monetary donations to ensure health care for everyone.

"To hell with the census!"

Before she could sit up, he'd joined her on the bed. The next thing she knew, he'd pulled her into his arms and was covering her wet face with kisses. Each brush of his compelling mouth against her cheeks and eyes broke down her defenses until he'd reduced her to pulp.

"You've been so brave out here, Heather. Everyone in Zocheetl loves you. They all look up to their Golden Mama. Only *I* know the sacrifices you've made. I know everything, *amorada.*"

She blinked. "What sacrifices?"

"Do you think I don't remember how you called this a godforsaken place after you arrived? Don't you know I've watched you work yourself ragged to fill the hours at great sacrifice to your health?

"Your reaction to your father's gift has just confirmed it. I wish I could let you get on a jet and fly home today." His voice throbbed. "But it would be much too risky now."

Dear God. Their marriage really had fallen apart.

Since their blowup at the condo, she'd done such a good job of rejecting him, he was feeling remorse for forcing her to come out to the Chaco with him.

Worse, he'd just told her he would let her go home right now if he weren't so worried about her physical condition. That meant he wouldn't stop her when the time came.

"Elana told me to go to bed. How sick am I?" she asked in a dull voice.

His hand stilled on her arm.

"Don't lie to me, Raul. I'm an O.B.'s daughter, remember. I've got toxemia, haven't I?"

"Yes." His voice grated.

"How long has my blood pressure been off the charts?"

"I don't want you worrying about anything, Heather."

"Have I been sick a long time?"

"Long enough," he whispered.

"So I'm going to have a cesarean?"

"Yes."

"Then the baby's going to be premature."

"If it were born tonight, we wouldn't have to worry. It's your health I'm concerned about."

His arms tightened around her. "Lie still, *amorada*. Relax. I won't let anything happen to you. Do you have any idea how long I've wanted to hold you like this?" His voice shook. Strong hands roved over her possessively, feeling every inch of her belly.

"*Dios*—the baby's so active! No wonder you've been restless at night. Have you thought of names yet?"

Her eyes filled with liquid.

"If it's a boy, I was thinking we could call him Jaime Ramon Cardenas, after your father and uncle. It would be a wonderful way to honor both of them. Jamie's a nice name in English, too," she added quietly.

"You must have been reading my mind." He smoothed some silky tendrils from her forehead. The merest touch sent a yielding feeling of delight through her body. "I wonder if you could guess what I've been thinking for a girl."

She kept her head turned away from him. "Probably not."

"Phyllis gave me the idea without knowing it."

"When was that?"

"At our wedding. Does that give you a hint?"

"No," she whispered breathlessly. Being this close to him was pure torture. She was in a flammable state. Despite knowing how he really felt about her, one more minute and she would be throwing herself at him.

Her pulse tripled when she felt him trace her eyebrow with his index finger. "I'll give you another one. Wedding Day at Troldhaugen."

She blinked. Her mind recalled the storyline from the Peer Gynt Suite. "Solveig?"

"Mmm…Phyllis told me your mother wanted to call you Solveig after one of your Norwegian ancestors on your father's side. But your parents honeymooned in England and your father preferred to name you Heather."

Her head whipped around until their lips were almost touching. Her startled blue eyes stared into his. "I knew Daddy picked my name, but I never heard about mother's choice."

His dark gaze settled on her mouth. "Do you like it?"

"Yes. It's beautiful." Her eyes slid away from his. "Excuse me a minute. I have to use the rest room."

Summoning all her strength she moved off the bed faster than she'd moved in months, straining some muscles. Raul, of necessity, had to let go of her. When she crept out of the bathroom a few minutes later, she found him standing in the middle of the hut waiting for her, his expression so bleak she hardly recognized him.

"I didn't realize my touch was literally re-pellant to you. Have no fear, Heather. I won't come near you again unless it's out of absolute necessity."

"That's not wh—"

"You need to be in bed with your feet up." He cut in as if she hadn't spoken. "It's obvi-ous you can't rest with me around, so I'm go-ing to leave. I'll have your lunch and dinner brought over from the kitchen. Is there any-thing I can do for you before I go?"

She shook her head in frustration. "You don't have to leave. This is your hut, too, Raul!"

"It's your hospital room now. Juan will be around later to check your vital signs."

On rare occasions, Heather had seen the for-bidding side of her husband's nature. But this was something else again. Before her eyes he'd transformed into the total doctor who manifested an innate authority and implacabil-ity she didn't dare question.

He piled extra pillows at the end of the bed. She had no choice but to lie down. When she was settled, he removed her socks and sneakers to examine her swollen feet. How embarrassing to let him see her in this condition, but it was too late now.

"Show me your hands."

She lifted them for him to feel. Almost three months ago she'd had to stop wearing her wedding ring because of swelling. He'd probably noticed it missing before now. She'd packed it safely away in a drawer.

When he'd finished his inspection, his hands took their time relinquishing hers.

"Am I a case for the books, Doctor?"

His searching gaze trapped hers. "You're going to be fine, Heather. The important thing is to stay lying down. With bedrest, we might be able to buy ourselves another few days."

"That soon?" Her voice could have been a squeak.

"Yes. Before the pilot took off earlier, I gave him instructions to phone your father as soon as he reaches Formosa and tell him to come immediately. I knew you'd want him here."

With that revelation, Raul left the hut.

Heather lay there in a state of shock. As excited as she was to think she might be holding their baby in a few days, it meant the timetable had been moved up a month. Soon she'd be flying back to the States, away from this world that had such a stranglehold on her heart.

Only a few precious weeks remained to be with Raul. Then would come the separation and ultimately, the divorce. But she couldn't fathom not belonging to him. She couldn't even fathom getting through the next few hours without feasting her eyes on him.

To live apart from Raul for the rest of her life was incomprehensible. It was like trying to contemplate nothingness, the opposite of existence.

She couldn't do it.

"Madre de Dios—We should be able to hear the baby's cries by now!"

Raul felt Dr. Sanders' encouraging hand on his shoulder. "Everything's going to be fine. Let's go back in your office to wait."

"I can't, John. I might be needed in there."

"Only as a last resort. When Heather was born, I was in such a state, Evan had to restrain me from barging into the delivery room. Let's let Elana and Marcos do their job."

Raul nodded. "Thank God you got here when you did. I know seeing her father before she went into the operating room was the best medicine Heather could have had at a time like this."

"I'm her old dad. She *has* to love me," he teased. "But it's you who makes her world go round, Raul. Believe me, it's for you Heather was willing to undergo this. That's the way love should be. That's the way my daughter feels about you."

"Not anymore," Raul admitted in a haunted whisper.

John scoffed. "What are you talking about?"

Raul was on the verge of pouring out his anguish when the unmistakable sounds of a newborn's cry rang out clear and true.

"*John!*"

"*I heard that, too. The suspense is over. Your baby sounds completely normal to me.*"

A few more minutes and Juan poked his head out the door. Raul knew every expression on his best nurse's face. He wouldn't be smiling like that unless everything was really all right. Relief bolted through Raul's body, leaving him dizzy.

"Congratulations, Doctor. Your wife says to tell you Jaime Ramon Cardenas has arrived. Seven pounds, twenty-one and a half inches. Dr. Avilar will let you know when you can come in."

Raul wheeled around, clasping John on both shoulders. "I have a son, John!"

Heather's father was beaming. "And I have a grandson. For being four weeks premature, he's already a big boy. I doubt there'll be any problem with his lungs."

Inhaling sharply Raul muttered, "I just pray Heather's all right now."

John patted his arm. "The best cure for toxemia is to have the baby. You and Elana made the right decision to do a C-section before her condition worsened. The danger is over. It's home free from here."

"I know."

"But you won't believe it until you can see Heather for yourself. I understand. Believe me I do."

"It's more than that, John."

"What do you mean?"

"I have this gut feeling she's going to leave me." His voice shook.

Heather's father laughed out loud. "You've been under too much strain for too long. Remind me to show you something later when you've satisfied yourself that your little family is coming along just fine."

"You can do that right now," Elana called to them from the doorway.

At the sound of her voice, Raul's heart leaped. He needed no urging to enter the room where he'd been operating for years. However this was the first time he'd crossed over the threshold as a terrified husband and new father.

The waiting had been agony.

But pure ecstasy suddenly filled his universe when he saw Heather on the operating table holding a tiny bundle in her arm with Marcos's help.

Tears streamed down her cheeks. "Marcos says he's perfect, Raul! Look and see for yourself."

"First I want to look at you, Heather. How do you feel?"

"I'm wonderful. Honestly!"

Even after everything she'd been through, she was keeping up the pretense for his sake.

"Go on. Examine your boy. You know you're dying to. He's so beautiful." Her voice shook.

Obeying a need beyond his control, Raul leaned over and kissed her lips. "So are you, *mi esposa.*"

"Not with my raccoon face," she moaned.

"Your mask of pregnancy will be gone in a few days," he assured her before his anxious gaze wandered to his son.

"With all that black hair and firm chin, there's no question he's yours, *Jefe,*" Marcos quipped. "Congratulations."

Raul eyed him solemnly. "Thank you for being here for Heather, Marcos. I'll never forget."

"It was my privilege. Now I think your son would like to meet his legendary *papa*."

With trembling hands Raul picked up the baby who only moments ago had been inside Heather's womb. Incredible.

He transferred his gaze to his wife whose eyelids were fluttering. "Jaime's got your nose and mouth, Heather."

"His long body is yours." She sounded drugged. Elana had given her a hypo for the pain. It had started to work, thank heaven.

Leaving her to rest, he carried his well-behaved son over to the table. John joined him. Together they undid the hospital blanket and examined his warm wiggly body that did look perfect.

"He's alert as he can be," John proclaimed with a telltale tremor in his voice. "If it turns out he doesn't have my daughter's eyes, you can always try for a blue-eyed one next time."

A shudder passed through Raul's body. If Heather had her way, there wouldn't be a next time.

Don't think about that right now. She's just presented you with a son.

As the mantle of fatherhood descended on him in full force, Raul looked down into the beautiful infant face so reminiscent of his wife's. Already a vision of the future that included the three of them had taken root and refused to be dislodged.

"Raul?" Elana whispered after Marcos had taken over the baby once more. "Tekoa and Pango are outside the door, anxious to talk to you."

He had to clear his throat several times. "I'll be right out. Elana?"

"Yes?"

He gave her a hug. "Thank you."

"As Marcos said, this was our pleasure. We all love the *Jefe* and his family. But I have a little confession to make. I was holding my breath, too."

"I would never have known it."

"That's good."

"I'll see what the men want and be right back."

He took his leave of Elana and walked out in the hall. The moment Tekoa and Pango saw him, they moved closer. He knew why they were here.

"Golden Mama is fine," he assured them. "She's given me a wonderful son."

They grinned. Tekoa said, "A son make more sons. That's good."

Raul couldn't help but smile. "That's very good, Tekoa."

Pango thrust a bunch of flowers at Raul. "Give to Golden Mama. She love flowers."

"She'll love *these*," Raul murmured, touched by their love for Heather.

The two men had guarded her ever since she'd stepped foot in the Chaco. When she saw their gift, he knew she would be delighted and make a special place for the flowers in her priceless collection. She'd involved the entire settlement in gathering specimens for it. They considered it a great honor.

Raul knew he'd fallen in love with an extraordinary woman, now more than ever. He couldn't imagine Zocheetl without her.

CHAPTER TEN

"You can't go home yet, Daddy!"

She'd finished nursing the baby and put him down for his morning nap in the cradle. It was a masterpiece of exquisitely carved wood. Raul had asked one of the men in the settlement to make it after he'd learned they were expecting. Her husband continued to shower her with gifts. It had to stop.

"I've been gone three weeks, honey. It wouldn't be nice to take advantage of Lyle any longer. He expected me back a week ago. When the mail plane comes in later today, I'll be taking it back to Formosa."

"Couldn't you get someone else to cover for you and stay one more week?"

"Honey—I've already told you I'll fly down again in two months and bring Evan and Phyllis with me. Right now you and your husband need time alone."

She averted her eyes. "No, we don't. In a week I'll be able to travel. You have to stay that long s-so I can fly home with you."

A long silence ensued before her father sat forward. "You mean for a vacation?"

"For good," she murmured.

He shook his head. "I don't believe what I'm hearing. While Raul and I were waiting outside the delivery room, he said something about his fear that you were going to leave him, but I considered it so much mumbo-jumbo because of his near hysterical state."

Swallowing hard she said, "He was serious. Our marriage was over before we ever left Buenos Aires."

"You're both painfully in love with each other so I'm only going to ask one question. Why?"

"You're wrong about Raul. I was the object of his desire for one night. Not a lifetime."

Her father got to his feet. "Raul isn't the kind of man to lock himself in a loveless marriage. Otherwise he would have made provisions for you and the baby, but that would have been the end of it."

"You're wrong, Daddy. Before he knew I was pregnant, he couldn't get rid of me fast enough after I showed up here."

"Good for him," he said unexpectedly. "He knew what a risk it would be to confine you to a life in the bush if you didn't take to his world. It isn't for everyone, honey. He had to be certain."

Heather couldn't understand why her father was taking Raul's side. "But he never had any intention of letting me live out here with him."

"What do you mean?"

"After the wedding, he took me to his condo in Buenos Aires. I didn't even know he had one. At first I thought he'd decided to surprise me with a little overnight honeymoon before we left for Zocheetl."

The tears started to gush in remembrance of their ghastly fight. Her father reached for her and put his arms around her. Before she knew it she was blurting the details, leaving nothing out.

"So you see, he doesn't love me, Daddy. But Raul's the kind of man who'll be noble to the end no matter how he feels inside. That's why I have to leave. So he can have his freedom.''

"*Good Lord.* This is all *my* fault,'' she heard her father say. Slowly he put her away from him.

She stared at him in astonishment. ''What are you talking about?''

"Sit down, honey. This is going to take some time.''

Heather did his bidding.

He stood in front of the bed with his hands in his pockets. ''I'm afraid I'm the culprit who ruined your marriage without realizing it.''

"But you gave us your blessing!''

"I also terrified your husband without meaning to.''

"How?''

"When Raul picked us up at the airport, we went to a restaurant for lunch. At one point Evan and Phyllis left us alone so we could talk privately.

"I started off by telling him I was glad to welcome him as a son-in-law, but I expected him to encourage you in your music. He told me you had convinced him that you wanted to give it up.

"I told him he was wrong, that you were only saying that because you were blinded by love. When the first throes of passion wore off, you would miss it more than ever. Then I confessed something to him I've never told anyone, not even you."

She blinked. "What?"

"When I met your mother, she was on the verge of becoming a concert pianist. In my selfishness I asked her to marry me anyway. She accepted. But I always felt that she'd sacrificed her career for me. When you came along and showed more promise than she did, I made up my mind that you were going to be given the opportunity I'd taken away from her."

"Daddy!" Heather got to her feet.

"I pushed you and pushed you with your piano, hoping you wouldn't meet a man until you'd had the chance to really establish yourself. But I'd underestimated the power of love.

"When Raul Cardenas showed up at Evan's house that night, I knew something significant had happened to both of you. There was a tension surrounding you and Raul that couldn't be ignored. The way you two looked at each other, you might as well have been the only people left on the planet.''

Heather would never forget that night, not for as long as she lived.

''I purposely broke the dinner up early, but it was already too late. I found Raul in Phyllis's kitchen with you and knew the man was totally smitten. It made me angry.''

''Oh, Daddy.'' Heather made a sound between a laugh and a cry before she ran over and hugged him.

''There's more,'' he admitted after letting her go. ''I made him promise he would do whatever it took to make certain you kept up your music. Then I made him promise something else...'' Tears glazed his eyes.

''What was it?'' she whispered.

''Long ago your mother and I decided we wouldn't tell you about her female problems because we didn't want you to worry that you might have inherited any of them.

''She had eight miscarriages. You were her ninth conception. We consulted a specialist who sewed up her uterus so she wouldn't lose the baby."

"You're kidding—"

"Not at all. That meant your mother and I couldn't have sexual relations throughout her pregnancy. But it didn't matter because we wanted a baby so badly. Before long there was another problem. Your mother had to go to bed with toxemia in her fourth month. She was very sick."

"What?"

Her father nodded solemnly. "I told your husband all these things as one doctor speaks frankly with another. Since I knew you would be living in the bush under more difficult circumstances, I thought that if he was aware of your mother's history, he'd be alert to any of the same problems cropping up with you.

"Honey—if the two of you haven't been intimate, it's because he didn't want to do anything that could harm you."

For a moment, the world stood still.

With her father's explanation, everything Raul had said and done since they'd driven away from the château made perfect sense. But she was too afraid to cry out for joy in case she was dreaming.

"Daddy—" she said with her heart pounding crazily.

A relieved smile broke out on his face. "Before I leave Zocheetl, I'd like to ask your forgiveness."

"There's nothing to forgive."

"Yes, there is. Franz shared your letter to him with me. It hurt to think I was so unapproachable, you couldn't come to me with the truth a long time ago.

"If I hadn't been so driven by my own demons, you and Raul could have had a normal courtship first. I'm so sorry, Heather. But I promise I'll never knowingly let you down again."

"You didn't! You haven't!" She shook him gently. "If it hadn't been for you, I would never have reached the point where I could win the Bacchauer and play with the symphony. Raul was in the audience. I wouldn't have met him otherwise. He's my life! It was all meant to be, don't you see?"

As they smiled at each other in perfect understanding, the door to the hut opened, causing both of their heads to turn.

Raul came bursting inside. He looked so forbidding and aggressive, she hardly recognized him. From the sound of it, he was out of breath as if he'd been running a great distance.

"John?" He stared straight at her father. "If you don't mind, I'd like to talk to my wife in private." The steel behind the words sent a shiver down her spine.

"Of course. I was just on my way out. I'll take Jaime with me." As he kissed Heather's cheek, he flashed her another message of understanding before he lifted the sleeping infant from the cradle and carried him out of the hut.

Raul let his father-in-law leave with the baby now, because there was no way he was going to let Heather and Jamie get on that plane with him later in the day. No way at all.

To his relief his wife was still wearing a robe over one of her filmy nightgowns. His tortured mind already had pictures of her and the baby dressed for travel, their bags packed.

"You're obviously upset, Raul. What's wrong?"

Flowing gossamer hair framed that exquisite face where her eyes blazed such a feverish blue, he felt himself drowning in them. The way she was looking at him... She was such a breathtaking sight, it caught him totally off balance so he couldn't think.

"I don't care what plans you've made with your father, you're not going anywhere."

"I wasn't planning to."

"You're my wife, and you belong with me."

"I know." She moved closer.

"Heather—" his voice rasped as a sweet fragrance emanated from her gorgeous body.

Something was different.

She was different.

"Honestly, Raul—as if I could ever leave you. Just the thought of you sends a continuous wave of desire through my body.

"Come here," she whispered with the same seductive smile that had enveloped him from the stage of the symphony hall one magical summer night long ago.

Maybe he was hallucinating. His heart felt as if it was going to burst its chest cavity.

"Don't be afraid, Raul. My father just confessed everything to me a few minutes ago. I now know why you wanted me to stay in Buenos Aires. I also know the reason why you haven't tried to make love to me. No woman ever had greater proof of a man's love.

"We don't need to be afraid of anything, my beloved husband. Not ever again." Her husky voice spoke to his heart.

"It was an arduous journey full of secrets and misunderstandings, but they're all cleared up now. We've finally arrived at the isolated haven you spoke to me about in Evan's study. That haven where we can make love, not only for weeks on end, but for the rest of our lives. How does that sound?"

Raul had no words.

On a groan he joined her on their bed. They cried each other's names as they reached blindly for each other. She wrapped her body around his, entwining their legs, kissing him with such passion he knew she'd forgotten she was still healing. Without the baby separating them, he was in serious danger of forgetting it, too.

Her mouth. He couldn't get enough of it. Her skin felt like velvet. As for the mold of her body...

When her hand started to undo his safari shirt, he checked the movement.

She raised wounded eyes to him. "What's wrong, darling? Or have I completely misunderstood." The tremor in her voice devastated him.

"You know better than that," he said in a fierce whisper. "I'm so in love with you I've been out of my mind with pain not being able to show you what you mean to me, *mi amor*. But your body's not ready for what I want to do to you. We're going to have to wait a few more weeks."

"But—"

"No buts, Heather. No more secrets. No more misunderstandings. I want my adorable wife body and soul. But I want you completely healthy first.

"When that day comes, we'll fly to Buenos Aires and let my aunt and uncle dote on our son while we enjoy a honeymoon. Then you're going to find out what it's like to be loved by a husband who's been lying in wait for you for over half a year, scheming and plotting ways to ensnare you until you were well and firmly trapped.''

''Oh, darling—Don't you know? I was trapped the moment I saw you standing there in the Dorneys's study,'' she admitted. ''Because of your letters to them, I was halfway in love with Dr. Raul Cardenas long before we ever met. All it took was meeting you.'' She moved her head from side to side. ''How am I going to survive twenty-one more days?''

''Like this.'' He gathered her in his arms once more. The world faded as they proceeded to kiss each other into oblivion. Time passed, but they were so involved with each other neither of them had any conception of anything except their need of each other. Raul would never have surfaced if he hadn't heard the unmistakable cries of their infant son resounding throughout the settlement.

A few seconds later Tekoa called to Raul in a loud voice from outside the hut.

"*Jefe?*" His voice carried. "Dr. John send Tekoa. Little *Jefe* wants Golden Mama."

As Raul reluctantly tore his mouth from hers, Heather groaned. "Poor Daddy. I know he wouldn't have interrupted us unless it was absolutely necessary. But did he have to send Tekoa? Thanks to his big mouth everybody in Zocheetl knows exactly what's going on in here," she grumbled before starting to get up.

Raul's chuckle had turned into full-blown laughter. "These people are more matter-of-fact about what goes on between a man and a woman. It's one of their most endearing qualities." He kissed the back of her neck.

"So I've noticed!"

He loved it when she blushed.

He loved his wife with an intensity that frightened him. "Our son sounds ravenous. I'll go to your father's rescue. Don't you dare move."

Her heart shone through her eyes. "*Never.*"

"Heather? Now that we've finished lunch, might as well come in the examining room and let's get your six weeks checkup over with. Bring Jaime with you.''

She stared at Elana in surprise. ''But I thought my appointment wasn't until the day after tomorrow.''

A mysterious smile broke out on the other woman's face. ''That's what your husband thinks, *if* you get my meaning.''

''Elana!'' she cried with excitement as comprehension dawned. Unable to get the whole business over with fast enough, she picked up her baby who was still dozing in his carry-cot and followed her friend out of the dining room.

It wasn't long before Elana made her pronouncement. ''You're in terrific shape and can start living a normal life again. Congratulations!''

''That's the best news I ever heard!'' Heather leaped off the examining table and hugged Elana. ''Raul's been in town consulting with the company that's going to build our new hut. He'll be returning before evening. When he gets bac—''

''Marcos and I will be on hand in case he goes into cardiac arrest,'' Elana finished for her.

A gentle laugh escaped Heather's lips. "You're horrible," she teased.

"I've been told that before. As for your son, leave him with me so you can go home and get ready for the big event."

Heather's eyes lit up. "You mean it?"

"Of course. I wouldn't have offered otherwise. Marcos and I have already talked about it."

"When did you plan all this?"

"For the past six months."

After the words sank in she whispered, "Six months?"

"Since he met a certain blue-eyed blond pianist on his quick trip to the States, your husband hasn't exactly been the easiest person to work with. Most of the time it's been "run for your life" around here. I'd say Tekoa summed it up best. Big *Jefe* needs Golden Mama now."

"He didn't!" She turned all shades of red.

Elana raised her palm to the square. "I swear."

"I-it's very kind of you to offer to watch Jaime, but—"

"But nothing. We don't have any seriously ill patients in hospital at the moment. Besides, Marcos still has to pass a few more tests. This will probably be the most important one to date."

"And then?" Heather cried in delight. Two of her favorite people were in love and needed to do something about it.

Elana averted her eyes. "And then we'll see."

"Jaime? Did you hear that?" she said to her precious little boy who had just awakened. "You have to be very good so Marcos can impress Elana with his fathering skills."

He immediately yawned and they both laughed.

She picked him up to kiss his cap of black hair. "They're going to take perfect care of you, sweetheart. In fact, they love you almost as much as your father and I do."

Her head lifted. "I'm going to miss him, Elana."

"I don't doubt it. But I have the strongest hunch that by the time your husband enters the hut later, you'll have something else on your mind. Come on, Jaime. Let's find Uncle Marcos.''

Heather watched her leave the room with her son who seemed perfectly happy to go with her.

''Elana—''

The other woman turned around. ''What's the matter? Don't tell me you're nervous to be alone with your husband—''

She let out a soft gasp. ''How did you know?''

''You're transparent where he's concerned. The day you flew in to Zocheetl, Marcos found me in the hospital. To quote his exact words, 'We have a visitor. She's in my hut recuperating. I'd give my soul to find a woman who loved me as much as she loves Raul.'''

''He said *that?*''

''Later, he said even more. Apparently when Raul barged in on the two of you, he was so riddled with jealousy, Marcos had the real fear he might just have to defend himself.''

Heather remembered. ''I didn't know Raul could act like that.''

"None of us did. That's when we realized the *jefe* was in love. Which is why you don't need to worry about anything. Love will find a way."

"Thank you, Elana. You're a wonderful person. One day I plan to return the favor."

She flashed her a quiet smile. "I'll hold you to that."

Though Heather felt a pang to see her precious baby disappear from the room, another part of her could hardly breathe anticipating her husband's return.

Thanks to Pango and Tekoa, who loved Raul and were always eager to help, all the preparations had been made by the time she heard the drone of the plane.

The flight from Formosa had never seemed to take so long before. As soon as he felt the wheels roll onto the ground, Raul jumped down from the plane and broke into a run, eager to show his wife the first draft of their house plans. He also had a letter to give her, which had come in the mail pouch.

It seemed that a certain plant Heather had sent to the university because she couldn't identify it, had turned out to be a new species. The botany department wanted to meet with her in person at the earliest possible date to talk to her about a name for it.

Filled with pride over her accomplishment, he couldn't wait for her to read the exciting news for herself. But every thought went out of his head when he opened the door to their hut.

His wife stood in the middle of the room, dressed in the long black evening gown she'd worn to play with the symphony. But there was a womanly change in her. The birth of their son had made her more voluptuous.

Candlelight flickered in the semidarkness. He saw its reflection highlight the gilt in her hair. Beneath that profusion of white-gold silk, twin orbs pulsated a hot blue so beguiling, he couldn't catch his breath.

Dios. What a sight.

She flashed him a haunting smile. It sent a powerful tremor through his body.

"Good evening, Dr. Cardenas. I'm Heather Sanders. Though we've never met, I've heard so much about you from the Dorneys, I feel that I know you well.

"Come in and make yourself comfortable." She drew him over to a chair. Her touch sent a current of electricity through his system. He sat down because his legs would no longer support him.

"I understand life in the bush can be very exhausting. Please—feel free to enjoy your meal. But try a little of this first. It will help you to relax." She poured him a glass of wine.

Raul didn't need a drink. He was already intoxicated by the sight of her. The flowery scent emanating from her body acted like a drug on his senses.

"It's true that I gave up my career as a concert pianist, but on occasion I still perform the private concert here and there. I understand you're a music lover, Dr. Cardenas. In fact, someone told me you have a real passion for Rachmaninoff.

"Tonight it happens that I'm in a Rachmaninoff mood. So I'll play two works that I'm confident you'll enjoy. Afterward you'll have to excuse me because I have a date with my husband. You see, it's the first night of our honeymoon and I don't want to miss a moment of it. You can understand that, I'm sure.''

The wineglass slipped from his hand.

Within seconds divine music filled the interior of the hut, transporting him back to that earthshaking moment when he'd sensed that the woman at the Steinway was his destiny.

Drawn by an urgency beyond his control, he moved behind her, but didn't slide his hands to her shoulders until she'd finished the last note.

''I feel like I did when I stood listening to you play the Brahms outside the door of your practice room in New York. My heart is thudding. My body's shaking. My whole being is on fire for you.''

She unexpectedly jumped up from the chair and turned to him, wrapping her arms around his bronzed neck.

''For as long as I live, I'll never forget New York. But I wasn't your wife then. I hadn't given you a child. I love you in ways you'll never be able to comprehend, Raul." Her breath caught. "I want to show you, tell you what's in my heart."

"You just did with your music," he whispered. "Now I'm going to show you what's in mine. Where can we go and be alone, Heather?"

Her body trembled. "Right here."

"You know what I want to do to you."

"Yes. I've been aching for you."

"Then come here to me, *muchacha*."